I, JUDAS

I, JUDAS

| A NOVEL |

JAMES REICH

SOFT SKULL PRESS

Library of Congress Cataloging-in-Publication Data

Reich, James, 1971–
I, Judas : a novel / James Reich.
p. cm.
ISBN 978-1-59376-421-0 (alk. paper)
1. Judas Iscariot—Fiction. 2. Bible. N.T.—History of Biblical
events—Fiction. I. Title.
PS3618.E5237I33 2011
813'.6—dc23
2011025223

ISBN 978-1-59376-421-0

Cover design by Sharon McGill

Interior design by Neuwirth and Associates, Inc.

Printed in the United States of America

Soft Skull Press
New York, NY
www.softskull.com

I, JUDAS

THE RIVER COCYTUS

He moved between morbid articulations of rock and dull signatures of slime, following the quartz-lined way of Virgil, the lantern-lit coils of Dante, down through the splay of fossilized vegetation, shoals of crystallized fish, a vertiginous landfill of microchips, pterodactyls, and religious billboards, compressed jungles, sedimentary cities, rotting wings of cinema screens, diving boards, neon, crushed statuary, ashen corpses like nameless buildings, upright or split or flattened, until he reached Cocytus, the lethal river of lamentation. Beyond this river lay another, Acheron, and beyond that Judecca, the plain of ice. The end of his journey.

The river Cocytus rolled slowly, each wave a frozen iron bell. His reflection beckoned from the luminous black water. He crouched and looked closer. Bruises bloomed through the skin of his throat, imprinted with rope, the blunt blue-black line of it gouged like a prison tattoo. He fingered the raised welts and scorched nebulae pulsing over his larynx. Crystals of frost sparkled on his goatskin jacket. He studied the frostbitten fingers that had counted the money, the hollows of the neck from which betrayal had sounded, the voice that had spoken seductions, the spiteful pout that had driven in nails, and the eyes that had now apprehended so many versions of himself that he could no longer account for the many apparitions he was blamed for. His shadow swung across the fractured surfaces of the glacier as he stood upright.

From within the water, voices rose, enraptured in grief, millions of souls bound to the eros of disappointment and the crude arousal of grief. An abandoned bark drifted toward him, as though strung on a wire. The river screamed and the bones of a thousand flying fish spattered against the ceiling of the cave. The small boat was crusted with ice. He stepped into it, and it began to float toward the point where Cocytus and Acheron merged, toward the dreadful plateau of Judecca, his home.

He watched as a dorsal fin split the cold film of the river, protruding slowly, frozen shards falling from it. The blue-black fin pitched in the aching torrent. It was metal, part of a machine pulled into the dark. Then he saw the taillights of the car surfacing and the rear section of the familiar Lincoln Continental. Drenched in frozen weeds, a woman in a pink Chanel suit once again crawled upon the smooth metal. The limousine and its castaway surfaced for only a few moments, long enough for the woman's screaming to fill the vault.

Then, it was gone, back to the slow drag of death, a diffuse red froth in its wake. Judas paddled through it, recalling the day that he and his brother Jesus had ridden into Jerusalem for the last time. From that journey he had known there could be no return. This was the same. He saw Sylvia Plath slumped against a block of ice that resembled a frozen transparency of her death-oven, posed on her knees, her pale cheek pressed against its wall, gorgon hair all about her cardigan shoulders. She maintained the attitude of a housewife eavesdropping through the walls. He saw George Armstrong Custer marooned on a blood-glazed escarpment, a gaping wound smoking like an ashtray where his heart had been, a whiff of powder drifting from his gun's last chamber. He saw eyeless Samson nursing his erection in the gray slush of the far bank. Judas appraised the suicides without judgment, for in the rootless coils of eternity he had been elected their reluctant monarch.

Frosted coffins shunted against one another in the timeless currents. At last, the skiff ran aground upon the huge sheets of ice that extended about Judecca.

He stood on the plain, in the shadow of the fuselage of a Boeing 767 that stood wingless and upright, part submerged like an image of a sinking ship; a giant spike from the frozen sea. Judas pulled his fleece tight against the Plutonian cold, the wind across the landscape of Judecca a glacial paean to the possibilities of suicidal death and betrayal. He looked at the numerals on the suspended aircraft: N334AA. One of the two planes from New York. Judas reached inside his clothes and tore a piece from the greasy pastry parcel he had made and filled with flowers from the trees that also bore his name, red petals spilling from the crust. He discovered that he could no longer ingest food. Wet clots of the oily pastry fell from his chapped lips and were rejected by his tongue as he coughed and gagged. The flowers of the Judas trees drifted like snowflakes as he wiped the grease from his trembling fingers.

Judas had lost track of time. How long had he been descending into the grievous earth? Time had ceased to function. One moment was decoupled from the next. He moved through its broken translucent sheaths as he did through morality, sometimes with nonchalance and at other times with a streetwise diffidence, a distant contempt at the corner of his mouth. Time was as transparent and measureless as the ice that surrounded him. It lent scenery to the stages of his rage, yet it was confused, conjoined, one moment projecting into another, with objects surfacing through the perverse film between them. It might have been hours; more likely it had been days. It did not matter. The effects were the same. He spat into the permafrost. *There is the speed of life*, he thought. He remembered the rotting rope breaking and how the mud beneath the tree had absorbed him, sucking him down like quicksand into a wet crack in the earth. The contractions had borne him to an opening, where he fell into a slick and jagged hollow. He had followed the slanting floor, blindly perceiving an impression of descending steps beneath his hands as he crawled, imagining the flow and progress of water and seeking after it. The raw steps grew more defined, and even the dense black thinned as he went lower.

Somewhere behind him, the agitated corpse of the dog Cerberus twitched and mouthed in what passed for moonlight. The three-headed hound had confronted him first in discordant overlapping howls and barking that caused small pellets of sedimentary stone to fall from the cave ceiling. Then it charged at him in an unraveling of ancient chains at its three collars and a fury of claws on rock. The six eyes of the beast—mastiff, pit bull, and jackal—glowed brightly and lit the flesh-sprayed walls. Its breath was a boiling, nauseating fog, and its carrion-wet fur stood erect along a deformed but powerful spine. Its tail whipped against the crude stone hall with the sound of breaking bones. Judas pulled his revolver from inside his goatskin jacket and fired on the horrific dog as it lunged toward him. His first shot missed, the bullet ricocheting into the catacombs beyond, as did the second. Suddenly, Cerberus reached the limit of its chain and the timeless shackles choked the dog heads and caused it to fall back. Here, Judas strode forward and shot each of them in a shattering of canines and palettes. The chambers of his futuristic gun had gasped and smoked in the chill as he ejected the cartridges. The dog whimpered from three wounded muzzles.

Some time after that, as Judas descended, a man with a mutilated ear stepped from the weeping shadows, waving a small, sharp trowel at him. At first, he took the shade to be the slave Malchus, whose ear had been severed that night in the Garden of Gethsemane, when Jesus was finally apprehended. As the weird light shifted about the walls of the funnel where they met one another once more, Judas saw that the man's thin skull was slicked over with linseed and soft red hair, like the peeling orange of lost Dutch royalty. His face was shadowed with paint and the worming palsies of infinite sorrow and madness. Crows pulled the skin at his eyes. Judas handed the gun to Vincent van Gogh and continued his descent.

At times he had exerted control, directing actors with electric shocks of his contempt or indifference, and at other times he felt that he was nothing more than a flickering ghost, a frigid shudder in the conscience where he might arise, summoned, dragged. He might be a whisper over a coroner's desk. Now, it did not matter that he desired otherwise or how bitterly he fought against it: his condition was one of simultaneity; he had entered into ambiguity and anachronism, existing in distortions, refractions, echoes, and caricature. There were millions of claims on his being. He was pulled apart and remade. His was the most exquisite corpse, the paragon of suicides. His name *Iscariot* meant "man of Kerioth" and that he was an outsider from the beginning, the sole non-Galilean among the disciples. This otherness also proved that from the beginning he was not a historical figure but a literary figure. He had been hijacked, pirated, fashioned, and abused. He no longer possessed any control over his image, his presence, recurrence, and attribution in space and time. Now, the rhythms and repetitions of his life were beyond his power to influence. Judas discovered death to be an endlessly transfiguring and distorting night.

The ice creaked beneath his crampons. He experienced himself as a fly on a museum case, beneath him a vast dredge and glassy cataracts of extinct megafauna, mutilated beings like homunculi, shreds of Atlantic cable, chrome hubcaps, ovens, the children of poets beating on windows, a suspended blizzard of smashed windshields, objects beyond his comprehension frozen and floating, structures of desiccated meat, lice, peacock feathers, and fur. He was walking on dead water, a sea of abstract desolation. Fissures allowed jets of burning gas to storm out of the surface.

His mind flickered with the infinite landscapes he had seen: a mosaic of presidential skull blowing in red fragments over Dealey Plaza, a babushka lady in the Dallas sunlight through a telescopic sight and cine camera on a mound of grass, bodies smashed in Pisa like a horror movie in the slabs of a de Cherico painting, fetuses in Roswell and the stench of Artesia's rotting cattle, flaming tanks in the tar pits of Los Angeles, barricades of dead horses and a cinnamon-haired general pushing his trembling revolver against his breast, the British Telecom Tower shearing in two like a broken horn, sex parties in Babel like a pyre of engorged flesh, the libraries of Babylon machine-gunned, Grumman Wildcats pouring like locusts into the Bermuda Triangle, bleach evaporating in the clinical halls of Glenside Hospital, women electrocuted in colleges of poetry, soft riots at rock concerts, Parisian hashish dens beneath the falling gargoyles of Notre Dame, tumescent rain forests with hanging monkeys, the star-worn care of nights on the flat rooftops of Nazareth.

This was before the escalation of love, dares, secrecy, and promises had made a straw prince of his friend, Jesus, and before the omens of rose moons and crows over the wheat field.

And somewhere in the distance, at the epicenter of Hell, Lucifer, the rebel angel, now monstrous, degenerate, and terrible, was also trapped in the ice, his massive torso yearning from it, pinned at the elephant tusks of his ribs, his bloodied wings ceaselessly beating to break free. As Lucifer's tears fell, the freezing wind from his wings transformed them to ice and held him faster. Gorgeous Lucifer, like Prometheus the thief of fire with his liver endlessly punctured and devoured by savage birds, suffered the fate of those accused of treason against the highest. Monumental, despairing, Lucifer waited for Judas at the center of the earth as though he were awaiting his Son. Judas moved slowly toward that confrontation, as he had done all his life.

THE GARDEN OF GETHSEMANE

One million cockroaches fell from the sun like bloody crusts of paper. The moon spread her uterine frost across the black and hollow heaven. We watched the slant of the stars as we had watched cold bright spittle spooling from the mouth of Lazarus, brothers of the tomb if not the womb, intoxicated in the vertigo of the crucifix, the swing of a bough inside a flash of lightning. Men were approaching.

My mouth moved inside the needles of his beard, not to identify him—because by this time, everyone knew Jesus of Nazareth by his somnambulant walk and dreaming words—but to *inspire* him for the last time, to breathe the remnants of my passion into him, and to finish what we had begun when we were children, to give him the strength to finish it. His brown eyes, as whorled and abandoned as snail shells, were closed; his pungent mouth disbelieving as the serpent of my breath hissed through his aching teeth, then passed over his tongue, into the shining purses of his flesh. I brought him here, constructed him from fleece, bone, blood, dust, wine, seed, straw, my occluded desires, my orphanage, the endless art of my fury. His disciples, his ineffectual mirrors, shivered between the soldiers and the knotted trees of Gethsemane. By this time, he could not resist anything that I suggested to him. It had been that way for so long that I did not have to witness him being led away.

THE BIRTH OF JUDAS

I might furnish you with opulent versions of my childhood. I might gift you the thirteenth-century iteration, as told by Jacobus de Voragine, the pulp hagiographer and archbishop of Genoa who in *The Golden Legend* merely superimposed me over the Egyptian myth cycle of Osiris and the Oedipal horrors of Sophocles; forgivable, for such is the chimera of my existence. My mother was named Cyborea and my father Simon, of the tribe of Reuben. Cyborea lay swollen on her pallet, sweating in her dirge of dreams. The time of my birth was near. The stars wheeled over the crude yellow home of Simon and Cyborea in Kerioth, and the earth was dry from drought. My mother, who also believed in witches, the power of lambs' blood, necromancy, gyromancy, and sinister agencies, was in the throes of a nightmare: I came from her womb, precocious and half-grown. With our umbilicus, I strangled my father, whose eyes bulged from his skull. Later, I would torment my mother, exposing myself, masturbating, and pulling the clothes from her breasts, until finally, she would relent and I would fuck her on the same pallet where I had been born, whose planks of bloodstained timber were the last images that my father had seen. Then, I would abandon her and her corrupted womb and prostitute myself to anything but God and become a golden young man, terrible, erotic, and cruel.

Such was her dream, and she took it to be prophecy, so that when I was born and the gruel of her body was still upon me, she locked me in a casket and cast me into the sea. This was like the assassination of Osiris in the iron maiden by his brother Seth, who abandoned him to the ocean in that sarcophagus, or like the setting adrift of Moses in his basket of reeds. Inside the floating coffin, for floating coffins are the vessels of parables like Ishmael and Jonah, be they of wood or whale meat, I was washed ashore on the island of Korkyra, which is also known as Corcyra, and Corfu.

Soon, aristocrats delivered me from the splintered box. They took pains to educate me at court and to train me, so that in Ionia I learned theatre and practiced the tensions involved in both hanging on to myself and occupying other beings across broken historical plateaus with borrowed masks and gestures. So, I could move within their rich absurd society. The island, the same shape as a lamb's amputated leg, was a place of olives, pomegranates, and narcotic vines; and there was myrtle, the sex scent of the Jews, its starry white petals and dark berries, and red-fruited arbutus, also with starry white blossoms, as eaten by bears in Madrid. It was a place of nymphs and intoxications of all senses. A pubescent girl from the extended family of the aristocrats snapped off a length of myrtle and showed me how it was like a penis, letting it loll between her lips, and rubbing it in the gauzy cleft of her behind, and sex began to possess me like drunkenness. We climbed into a tree and discovered ourselves engorged, swollen, and slick; silver petals and blossoms dripped beneath us as I entered her above the grove. Suddenly, she fell.

At first, I thought she had caught herself. Instead, her head had passed between two vines and her neck had snapped, the black fabric of her hair spooling over her face. I began screaming and was too panicked to climb down before the aristocrats discovered us, the body swaying in the boughs as though I had murdered her. I fled toward the sea and stole a skiff that was still loaded with salty fish. The winds from the Illyrian channel bore me away, fast into exile. After weeks at sea, near-starved and half-dead, I came back to Judea. Supposedly, I took a job as a page to Pontius Pilate. Some of that is how Jacobus de Voragine tells it. And there were other versions written and rumored across the empires before Voragine's Latin edition was translated and published in Bohemian and French editions.

No, the iteration that I prefer is the truth: the truth is that Jesus and I emerged together from the bell of a giant *pelagia noctiluca* jellyfish that was washed ashore on the Gaza Strip, large enough to contain our infant bodies in its luminous form. For a while, the medusa pulsed purple light upon the wet sand, as the waves pulled at its tentacles, pretending to suck it back out, only to force it ashore again. We crawled from the creature's mouth and lay beside the lantern of slime that was now dying upon the beach. In a flashing of fishing knives, torches, and filmy hands, we were retrieved. It is true that I was then taken south and raised in Kerioth, and Jesus in Nazareth. Later, when my parents moved us to Galilee, we were reunited.

KERIOTH, OR THE OUTSIDE

In Kerioth, we lived in caves that were excavated further from natural cavities worn out by the weather of the southern desert region. The caves were extended with stone exterior walls or with tents, as though Kerioth was a town splitting from within the earth. Rain was infrequent, and little grew. We ate grains and inferior olives and milked skeletal goats for cheese and ghee. Kerioth resembled a necropolis, a hive of tombs backing into the rocks from which undead workers would emerge and perform menial, exhausting tasks before returning to their graves. Cockerels picked over the dust, and the shrouds of the homes drummed in the wind.

It was in Kerioth that I constructed the first versions of the tale of Lazarus and of the resurrection of my brother Jesus, and it was also in Kerioth, with obscure memories of my birth, that I began to doubt my origins and to suspect that the people who called me their son were not my parents. Later, tourists like Mark Twain would pass through the sockets and ruins of Kerioth without even noticing it, en route from Beirut to Alexandria and the sphinx, after the tents had blown away and the goats had been killed. The cave homes were cool by day and were warmed by fires at night; sounds echoed about them, and the ghosts of conversations drifted out into the desert. From these conversations, I learned about the origins of the tribe to which I was supposed to belong.

The rabbis of Kerioth would dispute the incestuous crime of Reuben late into the hollows of night: did his intercourse with Bilhah, the maidservant of his father Jacob's second and favored wife Rachel, constitute a primal crime of incest? Mouths gaped and ranted in the fire-lit caves, beards singed or dipped into wine cups as the night wore on. They spoke of Reuben as establishing the archetype of the penitent, of how he might be something less than a traitor, little more than a rebellious son, and they spoke of his part in the conspiracy against Joseph, Rachel's first and Jacob's eleventh and penultimate child, and of things that I did not then understand. The tribe of Reuben possessed a labyrinthine genealogy that was prey to semantics and argument; it was tainted by incest and revolt, and as a literary construction, it was whence I had to emerge, the perverse outside, the distorted margins of myth. And all this sex talk was meat to the elderly rabbis, as much as it was to their acolytes; the distended surfaces of interpretation and linguistic discourse were a pungent veil over the vicarious thrill of imagining taking Bilhah, full-lipped and groaning, bent over a table or as she cleaned a floor; the details were lost and had to be recollected. What made the rabbis uneasy was the abstract fusion of the penises of father and son in the vagina of his wife's maid. They became indivisible in the erotic space and time of the maid; Jacob and Reuben were fucking one another by Bilhah's proxy. But she was just the maid. The intercourse of father and son with the same woman was merely an aspect of their Oedipal conflict. Such were the echoes that reverberated from the mouths of Kerioth.

We kept goats, and my childhood involved herding, feeding, milking, breeding, birthing, and slaughtering them. When it was necessary for goats to be slaughtered, I did this out of sight of the others that were to remain. I devised a killing place that was obscure and marked by a cypress tree surrounded by red earth. The goats were suspicious and would resist being led there, for they could smell the death in the soil. One goat I made special. He was charismatic and beautiful, and I set him aside in my mind and would allow him to grow old. His left hind hoof was misshapen. His hair was pale with strokes of copper. In the strips of his eyes, I saw great dignity. I would take him to the killing place with the animals to be slaughtered but always allowed him to return. The others saw him return unharmed, as though he had passed through the trials of death, and they placed a supernatural trust in him, and later they too would follow the strange goat to the outstretched arms of the cypress tree.

The roots of the cypress tree dripped down into the earth, bloody tendrils that were almost luminous through the soil.

They promised to penetrate the inverted belfries of hell, the oceans of the dead.

Palestine. Judea. Chateaubriand, writer, explorer, and lover of flesh, had at first experienced Judea with revulsion. The dust spoke of the coming neon, truncheons and suicides. Whenever he drank the water or deliberated on a piece of meat, he envisioned flesh and skulls torn apart by dynamite, a whirlwind of milk teeth and nails. The sun was like a tiger. A country is like a bath to die in, inviolate enamel, marble, metal; cartographies of watch hands, radar, lighthouses, cool ruins under floods of birds; rules to fill the bath with petals, to make wedding band and doghouse; wings fold in.

We left Kerioth beneath thunderclouds of suspicion. A boy was found dead on one of the lower plains where the children of the rabbis struggled to tend the dry crops. The boy's brow was split and bloodied, and a pair of his teeth shone in the sunlight that fell on the dirt. As soon as I heard the uproar of men and women crying and pronouncing the fatal blow to bear the shape of the runt hoof of my goat, I raced back to find him and to send him out into the desert so that the rabbis would not slaughter him. I walked into the rain, weeping. The man that called himself my father held his palm over my head, and the woman that called herself my mother struggled in the slow mire of our life. We took what few possessions we could carry. I thought of my goat, lost in the landscape of his crime and despair; his head fell lower, and the foothills turned blue. It was as though he was fading on another planet.

We struggled north until we came to the walls of Jerusalem. An aircraft carrier projected out of the south wall, strung with pulsing neon tubing, stars and stripes, a monstrous engine entrapped in the tendrils and tentacles of the chaotic city; a burlesque show kicked up sand from the vast deck. A jet fighter hung over the precipice, one wing dipping toward the dirt below. The carrier was named the USS *Eldritch*. I saw children throwing pitiful Molotov cocktails at the blackened hull before careening back through the split in the walls from which they had come like insects. Sanhedrin crouched and shrugged, cloaked in its shadows. The dancing girls stripped off their seamed nylon stockings and threw slingshot shapes, sending them slowly down to the desert floor like scented black angels. Legionnaires snatched at them and wiped them across their lips. In a clamor of black smoke and the sound of a machine vomiting, a Grumman Wildcat lurched from the deck of the carrier and clawed higher into the harpy dark. The metal of the carrier's hull ground against the city walls built by Herod, father of the tetrarch Herod Antipatros. For a moment, I pulled away from my parents and moved closer to it. Within the surface of the hull, in the bulkheads, conning tower, elevators, and gun turrets, were fused hundreds of contorted bodies, part encased in steel, part decomposing in screaming attitudes and torn uniforms, groping out of the architecture of the ship. Slowly, remaining outside the walls, we made our circuit of Jerusalem, where a bulldozer ploughed skulls into a grotesque hill of discolored bone.

"Look, Judas, they are preparing for a crucifixion." My mother licked her lips.

We climbed with the crowd for an hour, pausing only to buy kosher hot dogs and t-shirts. As we went, I whistled and sang beneath my breath my most beloved hymn, *Jerusalem*, by William Blake and Sir Charles Hubert Hastings Parry, and my eyes filled with tears as the first evening stars manifested over the city.

It was there, on Golgotha, where I first encountered the child Jesus of Nazareth. Our parents stood close to each other, but without word nor acknowledgment, so transfixed were they by the spectacle of the preparation and erotic swells of the crucifixions, but we children flirted and smirked as the first crosses of the evening were dragged up the hill. At first, I thought him to be an inauspicious wretch; his unblinking eyes suggested a perverse trust in the world. Regarding Jesus as we were then, as Roman soldiers kicked, spat, and slashed at the criminals nearing the summit, I saw the imprint of my goat, of myself, and of an amazing violence upon his soft skin. It was like the beginning of a love affair. That doe's unflinching stare and his gentle skin drawn over the imploring planes of his skull like wax are known from Franco Zeffirelli's *Jesus of Nazareth*, on the televisions of 1977, where our script was given to us by Anthony Burgess, a man consumed with regrets over creating disciples of another lethal, servile gang in *A Clockwork Orange*. I was written according to the evolving template of Judas as a handsome, soulful provocateur, the heartthrob with the anarchic smirk, undone by the politics of the Sanhedrin. That Judas' last moment is witnessed in a rustling sunrise, the chill boughs of dawn. There, dangling above the disbelieving money. Timpani rolls imitate thunder before the screen fades to black. In another version of myself, in the movie *Jesus Christ Superstar,* my substitute was a man named Carl Anderson. Carl Anderson has black skin. He was born in a place named Lynchburg, which means "city of lynching."

* * *

THE APOTHEOSES of crucifixions, the unforgettable ones, always transpire in the rain, when a creature's arms and shoulders and blood-flashed neck become an aqueduct of agony. It rained during our first crucifixion and our last, when we had pulverized Judea black and blue. The artichoke sellers pushed cursing through the crowd as rain began to fall, and a wave of joy broke over the crowd as the condemned men reached the place of skulls. Their naked, drooling shapes were drawn upward upon the creaking planks of the crosses, wrists and ankles shattered and impaled. They looked like albatrosses harpooned against the dark, men swinging in the masts of torrid ships, pouring sails of blood. Perhaps you have heard of the so-called *Philadelphia Experiment?* Morris Jessup committed suicide in 1959, in the slash pines of Florida, after years of obsession with the mysterious disappearance of a U.S. Navy vessel.

AKELDAMA, KINGDOM OF CLAY

When Jesus and I were seven years old, we would play together in the waste and rubble of Akeldama, which was also called Potters' Field. Akeldama was like an emptied city of scarabs where hard broken clay stuck out of the earth, where all the tiny buildings of broken earthenware were the mausoleums of birds and bloody weeds splashed across the surface of the dirt. We trod carefully, never ran, skipped, or danced there, for if we did we would gash our feet on broken vases and smashed crockery that the potters had abandoned. Instead, we picked our way over the remnants in the manner of strange compassionate giants.

"One day, I will visit that magnificent city," I announced, looking up and pointing into an ambiguous swollen space in the horizon.

"What city?"

"That one. The one in the far distance with the sunlight flashing from its roof tiles."

"I don't—"

"*You* don't see it. Of course you don't. Honestly, Jesus, sometimes I grow so impatient with your weak eyes."

"I'm sorry, brother."

"I am talking about the city between the rust-colored mountains." I jabbed my finger further toward it. "The golden minarets and wild buildings that are so beautiful, even from this distance. I wonder how many miles it is? Ah—" I said squinting, "that, that there must be where the King lives."

"Wait! I see it now. I was looking just away from it before. You're right. What a city, so golden." For a while, we two boys stared down the length of my arm as my sleeve shifted in the wind. The breeze disturbed the dirt of the field.

"Idiot!" I spat at him.

"What?"

"There is no city there! You are like a sponge. You soak everything up, true or false. You never know. I *always* have to tell you." I looked disgustedly at the tears dripping down Jesus' face. "*And* you are terrified of being wrong." I clapped my palm upon Jesus' skinny shoulder, grasping the cloth there.

Jesus sniffed. "Please, please stop teasing me, Judas."

"I'm sorry. You know that I only tease you because I am jealous. People like me cannot be people like you. That's how it is. I am the black sheep of a family that doesn't exist. You, you're the beloved lamb of tender parents."

"Maybe we could find your parents."

"Ha. That's funny. They live in that damned city over there, brother, or in this one beneath our feet."

"You're morbid, Judas. You'll murder yourself."

"Not before you do, little lamb."

Then I kissed him.

The Purchase of Aristocracy
and Broken Bones

In the midst of riches, there is ruin. The potters, who were brothers like us, became rich and, ashamed of their past, trashed the evidence of their former poverty, of their ever having been physical creatures who toiled with slimy hands to make urns. Their death urns were glorious and had borne the chaff of many reputable men, including Pharisees and soldiers. But when, as Zechariah tells, they received thirty silver pieces for their land, they renounced the physical world and became aristocrats. I, Judas, was inspired by this. Many of our childhood dreams took place in their field of broken clay. Later, I would pass this on to the carpenter. The carpenter was of the same grain as the rich brothers, and he too would turn away from his own splintered palms, toward abstraction and the callous righteousness of those who cease to credit the cloth and flesh of the world, and, like the potters, he would become a ghost in the looms and fornications of men.

Jesus and I spoke often of heroism, of sun-shouldered Ajax falling upon his own sword, of the tepid water around Socrates' goaty shins as the hemlock kissed his pores and gargled in his throat, and of Dionysus torn apart by his disciples. Later, we would have our own rituals of the vine and of breaking the body. We spoke of the vanity of Samson and of Hercules as we ate olives and spat stones. Seneca bled himself dry in our thoughts. Classicism had reached our shores, washed up in the scrolling waters of the sea, blown over our feet in the dust kicked up by the Occupation. Everywhere we were confused, as though caught in a storm too slow to be visible, one with winds that moved us without our knowledge and with immense irresistible power.

One day, at that same time when we were still boys, we watched a prostitute being stoned to death. With the first blows, her jaw broke off and hung slack in a pocket of skin. At one point, a Roman soldier drew near to the front of the crowd and moved to pull out his short sword to relieve her of her misery, but the mob held him back and might have killed him also, but for their fear. It seemed to take forever for her to die, and many stones. There was a smell like carrion, and a wheeling of crows that fascinated Jesus to the point that he was watching the sky when the last stone broke the woman's neck.

"How would we know the difference between a bird and an angel?" he asked. We played pinch as we went through the streets. "For example, if I heard a voice in my head while a bird was near, what should I assume made the voice?" The slow storm dust rolled about our ankles. "What if it had told me to pick up a stone?"

"I'd say that you were a hypocrite."

"And what if it had told me to stand up and shield the woman from the stones?" Jesus asked.

"Then you might be an even greater hypocrite."

"I wonder if it requires more bravery to save a life or to take one."

I told him: "Cowards tend to do both."

*   *   *

WE CAME, one night, to a moonlit escarpment, silver glints over the precipice and insects shrugging in the chill black. We took turns running toward the edge, our hearts cracking in the fear that grasped our chests, our bare, scabbed feet slipping in the spaying dust, closer and closer, until we became exhausted. I told Jesus that he was a coward again.

"Judas, you weren't *watching* me!" Jesus complained like a child performing to an absent father. "I was so close!" His lips trembled as he spoke. "I might have gone over the edge, over the world, spreading my arms out like a bird."

In my mind's eye, I saw him hurtling over the precipice, the knotted span of his flesh suddenly frozen in time, suspended in that hanging night, forever. I would think of it again during the night following his crucifixion, his passionate sprint into the paternal embrace of extinction. I would think of his exhilaration as he spread his imaginary wings over the earth. And later, it would seem perverse to me that any of his followers would want to wear the crucifix about their necks, since they do not with any other instrument of capital punishment or suicidal recklessness.

When we had thirteen years behind us, Jesus and I used to watch the prostitutes. There was a certain street where a sentinel dog was kept at either end, snagged on a short chain. Those who knew the street and the dogs made certain that when they visited, they palmed a chunk of raw meat to the dog as they entered. Otherwise, the howling and whining would make the whores disappear, as if they were sustained only by the leave of the dogs that chewed silence and let motes of bone and stiff blood fall like stars from their mouths into the dirt. We called the dogs Gog and Magog. After we had paid our tithe to the dogs, Jesus would always cup his hands about his nose, sniffing in the smells of the meat and the spittle of the animals. Once, as he skipped along beside me in the darkness, he pushed his damp hands toward my face and said: "Here, Judas, breathe in a whore's scent!" His eyes shone in the moonlight. I had never seen him so happy.

In later years, Jesus would still mingle with prostitutes, not because he was tolerant of them or fascinated by them or because he cared about them, but merely because he did not want them to be whores anymore, because he had become an aristocrat. It was not that his love or compassion extended to them. Jesus desired that they extend toward him, by ceasing to be that which later offended him. The street was a bell of ambivalent guttural music, and it was there we learned that the sounds of life, love, and ecstasy are so close to the sounds of death, weeping, and agony. We saw hip bones jut in the lamplight, women mounted like dogs, coins flashing like teeth.

Mary Magdalene was the youngest prostitute on the street and so the most notorious. Jesus was fascinated by notoriety and complained to me often that when we passed her, slouched in her doorway, she did not look at him. I told him that it was because he carried himself like a rich boy. This made him weep. "I am poorer than she," he protested. The dogs at the ends of the street shifted in the bloodied dirt.

I explained to him: "You might have a powerful father, who might have her killed if he knew that she had seduced his son. I don't know what it is with you, Jesus, but where you—in your vanity—feel the yoke of the world on your shoulders as agony, Mary Magdalene sees it for what it is."

"Oh," he said haughtily, "and what is that?"

"Adornment."

"Is that what you think, also, Judas? Tell me: don't you ever feel the weight that you accuse me of 'adorning' myself with?"

"Brother, I am more wont to feel it choking me, as though I had swallowed the world like a stone. People are suspicious of those who ostentatiously feel the pain of the world."

I dried his eyes with my sleeve. Such aphorisms and ideas I gave him, but he knew not how to deploy them, yet. Neither of us had quite decided who he was, or what he was to become.

"Then I will seem to ignore it, and become beloved of

women. Oh, and of men also, I forgot!" He scooped grit from the floor and tried to cast it into my face as we skipped away. "Come on, Judas," he sang, "we'll see her tomorrow!"

We left the dogs barking and the stars falling from the heavens.

The following night, we stood in the musky purple of the street, watching lamps extinguished and then lit again, and the men who moved with metallic shimmers, their coins luminous beneath the moonlight. Outside the place where Mary Magdalene worked, a house like a hollowed bone, draped in silk and sequins and cracked open so that the smell of marrow wafted into the night, we waited. We waited for Jesus' fear to subside. Finally, I grew bored, and I struck him across his flank and shoved him toward her door. He scuffed forward, and dust swelled around him. I watched her straighten her raw back and extend one of her hands to him, before I slumped inside the blackness close to the simple buildings on the other side of the street. He was gone for an hour. For that hour, I felt as though he were dead, and my heart was sick. The street had never seemed so silent and desolate. It dissolved until only a few lamps and candles remained. I felt as though I were hanging between the stars of the night sky, that I was a lightless constellation, asphyxiated by loneliness and knowledge. I was collapsing and sucking the universe in upon myself.

When Jesus emerged from her house, it was obvious that he had never undressed and that he and the whore had not made love. Without exchanging a word with him, I rose, shoved past him, and forced myself into the whore's quarters, slamming the door, locking it, and throwing her to the floor. She smiled up at me. I sodomized her until we were both bloodied and tearful. All the while, I could hear Jesus knocking feebly at the door.

THE DESTRUCTION OF THE TEMPLE

I can remember the first raindrops of the evening falling upon my lips. It was as though the heavens were full of salt and the land was raw, red and wounded. There was so much salt in the rain that when I looked, I saw that the sky was white. Can you imagine a sky as white as salt and the rain hissing out of it? Jesus' father, who was called Joseph, was shaking me by the shoulders in the middle of the market.

I had convinced Jesus to slip away from his parents and to visit the Temple with me. He was recalcitrant, of course, and entered like a donkey to its stall. Insects in black robes—the Pharisees, the Sanhedrin, the sects—negotiate the Temple, horrified by light and glass. For God is a boy with a glass, enthralled by transparency and torture. The Temple is a place of exposure, a more fatal lens than any sea, more blasted than any desert. Locusts walk on locusts in scorched wings and spastic limbs, which is to say that guilt is their honey. Beneath their hoods, they are skeletons dreaming of sugary flesh.

"What are we doing here, Judas?"

"Don't you want to see what happens here?"

"Oh, I know, prayer upon prayer upon—"

"Ha! You think you're cynical? Look at this." I showed him the Court of the Gentiles. His mouth fell open, and I told him: "It's no better farther in. Those men, on the blankets there, are gambling. And those are moneylenders. That man is a pickpocket. This one is a murderer." So it went. Soon, Jesus was calm and walked freely.

"Ah, I see why we are here," he said. "You want to see if holiness is the same as chaos and violence. You said that once."

"A white sheet exhibits more dirt."

"I remember that my father once bought a lamb to sacrifice. It looked clean, but beneath the fleece it was diseased."

"Your father either knows nothing about sheep or nothing about sacrifice."

Jesus hesitated. "Fathers don't understand sacrifice at all, but mothers do." At that moment, a Roman soldier pushed between us. "I'm certain that his mother misses him more than his father does."

"I have neither, remember."

"Then, at least you are free to create what you wish of them."

"My father's house is *here*," I said, and hit Jesus on his skull.

"And mine also, even if my mother is in my breast."

Later, we saw the Roman again. He was weeping. The insects in black robes had rejected him.

Jesus' parents worshipped me and treated me as their second
son. That is a lie. They regarded me as though I were a whore
at a wedding, uninvited, filthy, yet too dangerous to eject
because of my intimate knowledge of the other guests. Joseph,
the carpenter, knew that he was not Jesus' father and suffered
greatly from shame. This shame he fiercely unleashed upon
his craft, so that, soon, all he could fashion were the most
brutal of joints. He was afraid of me, but he was not so afraid
that he would not sometimes seek to beat me. My precocious-
ness infuriated him. It is true that I am a precise and prescient
judge of character. One afternoon, as I was drifting through
the sawdust of his workshop, I mentioned abstractedly, "We'll
all be making crosses one of these days." I felt his file slow in
the grain, and his brow knot and age.

Everything went black.

Mary, whom you will know as Jesus' mother, was a thin,
nervous woman with dove-gray skin. The choking secret that
she swallowed concerning Jesus' conception meant that she
spoke little to those beyond her immediate family. She told
me, though not directly, not with words, that conversation
petrified her, that her terror was that if she began to speak
and spoke for too long, then reality would spill from her,
flooding like blood from a slit wrist. In her silence, she prayed
that truth and reality would be expunged. When she drank
wine, she made certain to drink herself to sleep rather than to
confessional communion. Sometimes, if I found myself alone
with her, I would speak to her, to seek some new advantage
over her boy.

"Do you know about the wine cults of the Romans and the Greeks?" I asked her. She shook her head and nibbled at her fingernails. "Should I tell you, then?" Her gaze flashed around the walls of the room, where candles dripped and some cloths hung. I told her about Dionysus and the miracle of his birth, and I told her about his processions and of his being torn apart by his disciples.

"Gold, frankincense, and myrrh, and a star-fall more lighted than Lucifer. These luxuries your son claims to remember of the circumstances of his birth. Distortions. Nostalgia. The vine that gives strange memories and dreams that swim in fluid is like an umbilicus." As I said this, Jesus' mother moved her head in denial. The candlelight shifted across her features, and I studied the ticks and dilations of her fear. I went on: "It is predictable, a winding thread. With a few more pulls in one direction, I might find out about Jesus' birth. In the other direction, far ahead of us, are the lessons of the vine."

"What is there?" Mary asked.

I ignored her question but told her: "I know that Jesus has had a mirage burned around his birth. I recognize shame when I witness it. If you had ever really held gold in your hands, then we would never have met. Me, a runt from Kerioth."

Jesus' mother laughed nervously.

"Don't be afraid. Jesus is my friend. His interests are mine. If the old mirage wears thin, I will make him another, embracing him like an angel."

"You are a good boy, Judas."

I explained: "One must teach with the vine and make new life with illustrations and distortions of nostalgia. Perhaps you will find that Jesus is a miracle, after all. That would be no shame, would it? Drink up."

Mary drank the wine. I watched her lips shaping to speak in the half-light as though they were animated by pulls from a fishhook. At the same time, her lids began to fall across her reddening eyes. She was like so many mothers who ward against truth with silence and sleep.

THE FLESH EATERS

I sat with Jesus in an olive grove, violently spitting stones at shadows. When I had eaten the flesh from each olive, I would roll my tongue around the stone so that I was holding it in a tight tube in my mouth before inhaling deeply through my nose and blasting the air back out through my tongue and parted lips. The kernel thudded from my mouth, shooting into the gravel. Jesus concerned himself with plucking the thin hairs that had begun to push out of his skin, making pinchers with his thumb and fingernails. His eyes were red from the pain and his nose dripped as, hooked around like a crab in his dirty clothes, he ripped tiny black threads from his armpits and groin. I imitated his father's voice: "You are becoming a man, at last."

"I don't want to," he hissed, licking spots of blood from his nails.

"You have no choice." The sound of my hand across my jaw hissed back at him. "A face for carpentry and crosses, a cock for crowing at whores, and armpits to spread out in the sun."

"Do you have anything to drink? I'm thirsty."

"Here." I passed him my gourd. "Only, leave me some." He unstopped it and raised it to his lips. I watched his cheeks fill and his red eyes widen in shock.

"Wine! Where did you get this?"

"Pilate's decanter."

"Liar."

"I can't tell you where I got it because I made it."

"You don't know how!"

"Well, brother, you start with, um . . ."

"Yes? Judas?"

I pretended that Jesus had bettered me. He was getting the hang of it. He drank more wine and handed the flask back to me. We continued to share it until it was empty, and our heads ached in the sun. Jesus felt his feminine shoulders melting into the hard and prickly bark of the tree where he reclined like a prince, long-haired and beautiful. We were in languor. The tree whispered his old trade, his father's work, back into his flesh. His mother's voice was in the breeze. Yet, he heard neither as I lay down with him. His lips were wet and insipid; they were like spoiled fruit. He listened to the gently conceited echo of his self as the wood folded like a fleece around his neck and back, and a dutiful sleep descended for him. His robes lapped about him. All was peaceful with him. I could hear him speaking, waking me. "Mastery is not convincing others of what you know, but convincing them of what they do not."

The Psalm of Iokanaan

One summer, we went out to see the Baptist, whose name was John. He was singing as he stood in the flowing water. His voice was crude and nasal. This was before, as Oscar Wilde tells it, his imprisonment in a cistern, before the dance of the seven veils, and before the Baptist's head was hacked from his body.

"He holds them beneath the surface of the water for a long time, Judas," Jesus said.

"If I were to strangle you for a while, you would see sparks and angels, too," I explained. "It's the same thing. Actually, I love the Baptist, because I can sit over here on these stones and feel the ichors screaming in his blood. Do you hear that thin whining sound, above the river? If we met him in a silent street at night, the noise from him would split our ears. That is how I feel God. God is in my intestines, like a knotted rope that sometimes reaches out into my flesh and whips me."

We watched as he lifted his face to the sun and pushed another head through the froth of the river. The man came up gasping and full of terror, as though he had fallen from the sky and survived.

"Shall we move closer?" I asked.

Distortions of John's appearance are witnessed in films, paintings, and novels. In fact, he was tall, muscular, and handsome. One cannot stand in the flood of a river forever without powerful legs. His torso was like red marble, the softness burned from his skin by the blazing sun and the motions he made from his waist. He sang mysterious songs as he worked, rocking in a tumult of desperate bodies, pushing the pointless heads beneath the cold mirror of the river.

John the Baptist was much older than the two of us. When he finally stepped from the water, as the last of the gaping men and women struggled back from the river in their bare feet, across the stones to where they had left their sandals and clothes, the gibbous moon sent silver across his body. His hair was slick and black across his shoulders, and his jaw was as regular and brown as a book. Indeed, it seemed to me that his thighs were full of thick and struggling fish. As the years passed, Jesus and I would often visit him at his time of rest, before his scant sleep, but this was our first encounter with him, and we were much afraid. He walked in pensive circles about his small fire, which lapped between a skirt of stones. He could hear us breathing in the darkness, watching him.

"Do not be afraid of me," he said.

"Don't you wish to rest?" I asked him, swigging at the wine we had brought with us.

His laughter was full of patience. "Judas," he said, and I was astonished that he knew me, "the river is constantly in spate, and I am constantly still within it. I stand against the flow and have stood there, against it, waiting, all my life. When I leave the river, for a few moments before I am able to sleep, my soul cries for anything but stillness. My legs desire movement. In fact, were it not for God's will, I would run. I would flee the river."

"Jesus is much the same, aren't you, Jesus?" I said, and Jesus muttered something, pulling the gourd out of my grasp and swigging from it. I realized that, of course, the Baptist must know my name since he too had entered into anachronism and ambiguity. John had become stasis, patience, resignation, and death wish. His work was suicidal. He might have walked away, ceased to bring attention to himself, but there he waited, anchored to the stubborn river that flowed as if all things were inevitable. Even as we told our stories and listened to the locusts shifting in the desert, I felt the eyes of Herod's agents upon John, watching from behind mounds of shale. We were a funny trinity, shuffling around the fire. "Look at us, like brothers." I watched John's thighs and thought of Dionysus, the fetal god nourished in the thigh of Zeus, the old sky god. After a while, John ceased pacing, and we all lay down on the clammy earth, staring at the night and becoming drunk.

"When you sleep, what do you dream of, John?" Jesus asked, passing him the wine.

"Why, I dream of the river. Do you see those stars that look like the river, or those stars that look like a spine struggling to remain straight in the river? At a certain point, symbols begin to dictate the universe, and we become subservient to them, and sometimes we ourselves become them. A thing becomes necessary because it sustains the symbolism that suggested it. Do you understand?"

"I'm not certain." Jesus scratched his scalp.

I explained: "What John is saying is that the universe flows backward from poetry, rather than poetry being made of the universe."

"In the beginning was the Word," said Jesus.

"Yes," John told him, "we are intoxicated by symbolic structures. Every time that I baptize someone, there is a moment when they kneel with their shoulders submerged in the bright shining water, and do you know what I see then? I see a head on a plate. I see heads on silver plates, over and over again. It is burned into my brain. I know where I am going. Isn't that funny? And if . . ." he let the word hang, its feet dangling over the dirt as he put his arm around my shoulder, "if we can make one thing resemble another, one story resemble another, then we can strut the earth with the arrogance of gods."

JUDAS ISCARIOT, DELILAH, AND THE
SUICIDE OF SAMSON

At another time, I was called Samson. Even as a child in the wasp-infested town of Zorah, west of Jerusalem, I wore my hair long and flaming about me, and my skin bore the red glaze of the sun. I was vulpine, petulant, and mighty as a rose-colored star.

Now, Samson had been enslaved by the Philistines and was prey to a woman voluptuous as quicksand, her tar-black tresses reeling in the breeze like copulating serpents, her ankles nubs of ivory and her brow of awful white, her lips a red smear across a menstrual moon, everything glowing, radiating the ornate gifts of her sex. Samson dreamed of crucifixion beneath her painted fingernails, her hips working on him, a demon exhausting a horse. Samson rolled like a boulder in his dreams. The pallet where he slept creaked beneath him,

and his sheets drifted aside, revealing a granite giant delin-
eated by the moonlight. The halls were silent, save for the
coughing of the Philistine sentinels in the cold night or the
scrape of a spear shaft on a flagstone. Since his capture, he had
also fallen further under the luxuriant spell of the Philistines
and their arts than he had been as a young man. He touched
vases, imagining cool breasts beneath his palms. He traced
smooth facets in the vaginal walls of the Temple that was also
his prison. His desires, his bulging eyes, had always marked
him out, even as a young man.

This woman was not the first Philistine woman he had desired.
At seventeen, his wandering eyes had taken him to the seaport city of Ashqelon, to the north of Gaza. He encountered
her between fishnets and rocket shells, flaming tires and effi-
gies. A teenage boy had hesitated in front of the coffee shop
before detonating, smithereens of glass and torn flesh sending
a corona over the markets. From the rubble and olive shreds of
skin Samson had pulled the young woman. Like him, she was
a tourist, but she was from Timnah, closer to Jerusalem. They
shivered on the sandstone ramparts and watched garlands
being hung about the necks of metal bulls that remained since
the Canaanites. Since Samson was vain and easily swayed, he
decided that he should marry her, even without knowing
her name. When he returned to his home, she remained in a
hotel that overlooked the sea. In Zorah, he lusted for her and
raged against his parents. Samson's father was named Manoah.
Manoah was more afraid of the world than he had been before
the birth of his son, since it was surrounded with auspices of
angels exploding in fire and a disemboweled goat swinging

beneath the tree in his courtyard. Manoah relented and told his son to return to Ashqelon and marry the girl.

When Samson was a mile from the seaport, he felt a terrible blow fall across his ear, almost tearing it from his head, and a claw that ripped into his cheek and nearly put out his right eye. It was a Persian lioness, stunning and golden with violence. Samson opened his mouth and brought it down upon her muzzle, and gripping one front leg and one rear leg, he tore the animal open, splitting the hide as though it were paper. Then he collapsed in pity and grief, for himself and for the lioness. As he wept, a cloud of wasps filled the open carcass with spoiled fruit, flower heads, and honey from a beehive that they had destroyed. In the gore, they made a crystalline cave of bright sugars. He made a gift of the sugars to his bride, but each wasp gilded his guilt, his awful strength, and his fear of himself.

A delirium fell upon him. He became morbid, and obscenities shadowed his thought. He sought provocations and murders, spoke in non sequiturs and riddles, set up his wife as a golden heifer, and in a river of strange killings, the vengeful Philistines poured tar upon his wife and her father and set them aflame. Samson dipped the tails of one hundred foxes in the same tar, the tar that mended the fishing boats of Ashqelon, and set the foxes burning and barking through the Philistines' wheat fields. The cries of the burning foxes could be heard far out to sea, where skiffs rolled and lamented. And as men, women, and children poured from their benighted homes to extinguish the flames, he tore their torsos from their hips and smashed their legs against the ramparts and great arched gate of the city, as he had treated the lion. Then, as a man awakening from a drunken fever, Samson fled toward the bloodstained light of dawn. Exhausted, he came to the rock formation of Etam that rose like a majestic city of bone toward the Judean sky. His breath drew blood from his lungs, and his huge muscles were sodden rope under his skin. And it was with pristine ropes that the Philistines finally captured him there. His last act as a young man was to slip from the knots and massacre one thousand more with the jawbone of an ass, tears pouring from his bulging eyes, his skin radiant as the sun with blood and his long hair streaming about him.

He took solace in whores in Gaza but was infamous everywhere.

By the time he met Delilah, he was thirty-seven years old.

"You will not take wine?" she crooned like a junkie over a spoon.

"I am bound by my Nazarite oath."

"For a Nazarite, you have associated with many, many corpses. You have even taken sugared fruits from a cadaver."

"The oath was given by my father, before I was born, and it endures, my strength with it."

"Therefore, your hair is long, because you are forbidden to cut it."

"Yes."

"You have broken most of your oath already, I think, my necrophile." At this, she let her transparent black raiment slip from her breasts, and her red lips opened. Samson felt himself to be staring into a galaxy of sheens and glitter, of wet and rolling flesh, of erotic tombs and the afterglows of sacrifice.

"Should you cut my hair, I will be deserted by God."

"There is no God, my sweet." Delilah gestured into the candlelit room and the shadows thrown from the roaring fireplace. The lovers lay on a series of goatskin rugs. The wine goblets shone and fumed. "Look at these walls, the images and flatteries. You are in the Temple of Dagon, the god who was supposed to have flapped impotently on the sand before the ark of your Noah. The people here no longer know whether Dagon is a grain god or a fish god, and if he is a fish god now, it is only because we are closer to the sea. Now, let me help you with your lion's mane."

As his hair fell about him, and Delilah moved the soaped blade across his scalp, Samson was enervated and destitute. The angel of fire and his Lord deserted him. He felt like Seneca in his bath, as though his very blood were draining from his body. Delilah climbed upon him. He saw stars, foxes, and constellations of himself. She sucked on his near-flaccid cock until he ejaculated without joy or expression. Then, she put out his eyes with a glowing poker from the fire.

Now, blind, Samson felt that his life had already been extinguished. He moved in the coal-black as a corpse in the channels of the earth. He fell against the Philistine furniture, stumbled in the ornate catacombs of the Temple of Dagon, and although his tear ducts were gone, he sobbed with despair and the certainty of a sacrificial bull. When he could finally bear to touch the sockets where his eyes had been, Samson found only scorched anemones and appalling tendrils and flashes of skin that had fused with his face. The wounds were septic and burrowing into his brain. The other thing that he felt for was the stubble of red hair upon his head. Now that his eyes were such a horror, no one noticed that it was returning. For days he moved about the Temple, calling for Delilah. Finally, Samson resolved to murder himself, and everyone else within the confines of that darkness within him and without. The Philistines held a panic festival; all he knew was the heat, the noise and the whirlwind of it. Somewhere inside the vortex was Delilah, men and women collapsing in and out of her. Samson looked in vain for the image of it in his mind. When he finally found it, it was as though he was staring his death in the face. He saw Delilah. He found himself between two pillars . . .

This conjunction with Samson, one of the once-heroic self-killings of the Old Testament, was the first instance in which I, Judas, became aware that a composite of my life and death had become a lens for the reappraisal of the lives and deaths of others. Something about my death with Jesus of Nazareth had consequences that other deaths did not. The sensations of being thrown into another being return to me, yet the sensations are not entirely physical; they are aesthetic, moral, a manifold judgment, a sense of being watched, of being the ghost and the haunted. The sorrowful transgressions alleged against me are contracted in one brow, and now through compulsion I am seen in others, and through compulsion, therefore, I attend. The world, before and after me, is strangely tainted. This is not fair to any of us. Claims of my preeminence are false. I remember that Jesus was being interrogated:

"They say that you are a king? Are you a king?"

"I am what you say that I am," Jesus answered.

Jesus was wrong.

To be, or not to be . . . It is the most significant question of all. For a moment, an ice storm breaks glass against my face as I am back on the frozen plateau of Judecca that is at the eye of Hell, the subarctic sea behind me. There I am, as though in a dream, opposing, ending.

THE FIRST DEATH OF JESUS OF NAZARETH

The voice of my brother was calling me from my sleep. I awoke on the bank of the river where John the Baptist slumbered beside the embers of his fire. It was the dead of night. My mouth tasted disgusting from the wine. At first, I could not open my eyes. I had been dreaming of strange elevated tracks of metal, coiling like serpents through a monumental city whose buildings blasted toward the sky. I recognized it as New York.

"Judas! Over here!"

Jesus was standing in the river, and the moonlight on his denuded body gave him the appearance of a figure carved from pale wood. The water foamed violently around his hips. I could see that he was struggling to maintain his footing in the torrent of river and darkness. Eels, weeds, and slime moved against him; stones receded like razor crabs; distant lightning.

"What are you doing?" I called to him as I rose and hurried across the shale to the edge of the water. It was startlingly cold.

"I'm going to baptize you!"

"No, you are not." I tried to call to John, but the Baptist could not hear me. His huge satyr's legs moved languidly within his dream, and his sex stood out, as red as a dog's. I knew that he was dreaming of Herodias' greedy daughter.

"Look at me, Judas! I am like a fisherman. I can fish you!"

"You can barely stand!" I took a stride into the river toward him.

"My feet are bleeding," he laughed.

Something in his eyes changed, just at the moment when he knew he had exposed himself, uncalculated, to the vicious lens of the universe. Some years later, I saw it again. I was in Greenwich Village watching a woman strip in a bar.

Suddenly, Jesus was swept away, and I found myself running down the jagged banks to reach him as the current dragged him under and through frozen sheets of mortality, his body careening through glass. I ran with my soul exploding in panic. My flesh was as a swarm of bees. I moved across the surface of the crashing water and took his hand as it projected through the film of the river one final time. My face passed through knots of weeds.

When I pulled him out, Jesus was dead.

His blue-gray corpse lay bloated and naked on the bank as I forced my hands into his mouth, dragging out hanks of slime and filth. His hair was filled with grit and snails. I pressed my mouth to his and exhaled hard into his lungs. He began to cough and vomit as I pushed my breath inside him. The Baptist went on sleeping, as though we were his dream.

"I thought I had lost everything!" I told him. "For a moment, everything was undone, and we had failed." Jesus lay like a fish on the moonlit stones. He was translucent with death, yet I had revived him.

"It is a miracle," he said.

"Swear upon your life that you will never speak of this to anyone."

In those days, I knew not to trust him, but I did not know how his soul would spread and infiltrate by word and rumor, how these secret things would be retold by tangent and distortion. I was his commander still. Sometimes, when I recall these episodes, I am struck by our childishness, our ways of finding trouble, as if a mission like ours could have only been born of children, of recklessness. The child's love of danger is called faith. These were the days before my name was lightning striking the neon dusk of Hollywood and orchestras crying out in shame.

THE PIGS

Once, we were hired to drive some pigs from market to their new sty, in the purple evening foothills, from where Galilee glimmered like a coin. Aaron, the farmer, a hypocrite who sold unclean animals to the garrison, had promised us such a coin and a sip of wine, should we bring all of the dozen swine to his farm. He could not do it himself, because he was weak. "My shins are weak as candles. I can't hurry across the stones in this heat," he told us.

"Don't worry, master," Jesus assured him. "This is the kind of thing that Judas and I do best."

When Aaron had gone, hobbling with his cane, I turned to Jesus, saying: "Master? What's this 'master' nonsense, eh?"

"He's the one with the coins, Judas, or did you forget?"

"I like this new insolence of yours, brother. Did you get it when I brought you back from the dead?"

"We're of one breath, aren't we?" The sun was behind his

head, a blinding corona spilling out. The pigs were noisy and panicked as we drove them through the narrow streets. We beat them with sticks and cried at them. Jesus had a small goatherd's horn that he trumpeted sometimes.

He tried to trip one of them by putting his ankle beneath its back legs. One of its hooves hit his knee, and he became even more enraged. "Let's drive them into the sea! Filth. Filth!" Spittle flew from his mouth. "This one is like my father, this one is like my mother, this one is like Mary Magdalene, and this one is like a rabbi who is always masturbating, and this one a cowardly soldier, and this one is an idle fisherman, tax collector, fiend! They are full of ugly spirits." So it went.

By the time we reached the sty, we were spent, and the pigs were panting and heaving in the dusk, swaying through the small gate and slumping in the straw and dry soil. I poured water on them from their trough and fetched more for them to drink. I felt disgusted by the way we had treated them, even though some of it seemed necessary to get them to move between the people, dogs, carts, stalls, and din of the streets. I pushed their food at them, hoping that they would eat and recover from the driving. One had a trickle of blood coming from its snout. The others were making terrible sounds, the kind of sounds that a fish might make as it lay in a boat staring incredulous and mad into the sun. Jesus sat on the fence, grinning. When Aaron saw his pigs, he was distraught and made to raise his cane at me.

"No, master! I tried to help!"

He stopped, partly because he believed me and partly because he feared for his balance as the cane swung up around his ear.

"What in the name of God did you two do with these pigs?"

"It was Jesus, sir."

"Answer me, boy!" The old man turned to my brother.

"Your pigs are unclean," said Jesus, lolling down into the sty. "And he," he pointed at me, "is a traitor. He was crueler than anyone to these animals, and now he is full of self-pity and remorse. It makes me sick."

It was the first time that I had heard Jesus lie, and he lied about me. Later, as his mood flattened and he became melancholy, I understood that the transgression had come at great cost to his conscience. He had inflicted a wound upon himself. I sought to console him and gripped him to my pulsing breast after we had retired to a rooftop to sleep. Yet, if I were to make of him what I wanted, Jesus would need to inure himself against the bleats of a false conscience and to learn how to incubate falsehood in his heart, to deceive himself as well as others. The hooks and lines, the vines and intoxications of an ineffable god would thread through his ribs, inspire his lungs, and confuse his vision with briar, until the fisher of men and the envoy of the great deceit would be inseparable in him. He who was meek, I would make mighty by deception. He would believe such things of himself that only a drunkard may dream. He had also betrayed me and called me traitor, and I was impressed. For as much as accusations of betrayal are the refuge tongue of the weak who fear change, they are also the currency of the entitled that believe that nothing can move against them.

JUDAS ISCARIOT AND THE
SUICIDES OF VINCENT VAN GOGH AND
GEORGE ARMSTRONG CUSTER

The second time that I was born as Vincent van Gogh, it was on March 30, 1853, precisely one year since the first abortive attempt, when I was hung in the noose of my mother's umbilicus and came out stiff and blue as a tile. I am the Judas child of my own memory, the strangler of my own conscience, an endlessly looped half-truth. Time to remember my life then. When I died again, I was thirty-seven years old, the same age as Samson, my hair as short and flaming and my strength as desolate.

1860. Groot Zundert, the Netherlands. The old fireplace of our home was surrounded with Delft tiles. The flame shivered and meandered before my eyes and cast beautiful shadows across the blue illustrations on the tiles like a sailor's tattoos at sunset, rippling with exhausted flesh. These pictures were among my first stories: the tale of Saul falling upon his sword in suicide after the black magic of the Witch of Endor and defeat at Gilboa, his armor bearer following suit. Saul murdered himself like Ajax, and Ajax had lost his mind like Samson and had gone thrashing through a flock of sheep with his weeping sword. My first measures of men were these; narcissists hanging between the hemispheres of their own skulls, erotic, violent, and insane. I imagined their luxuriance, the feeling of their orgasm defeating their mechanisms of self-protection; they rolled in their concubines like foxes in carrion, and so was my desire.

In my earliest childhood and at boarding school in Zevenbergen when I was ten, I suffered terrible dreams. I saw my brother Theo, or one of his remote children's children, shot in the back eight times, the red fish gape of his slashed throat, and knives plunged into his body like a crucifixion and almost two hundred years passed in Amsterdam, his head lolled back under the remains of a starry night; and I decided that strange deaths and betrayals are all around us, a million martyrdoms to keep the sun and houses and wheat fields yellow, and many are the myths perpetuated about us. Once, I held my left hand in the flame of an oil lamp to make myself forget everything.

Isleworth, June 25, 1876. In April, I had been in Ramsgate with the Reverend William Stokes before moving on to the borough of Isleworth, within the span of London, tutoring and composing sermons at the school of the Reverend T. Slade Jones. Isleworth had been a place of monasteries and orchards, but now I skulked in the shadow of the soap factory on the London Road and sought out gin and solitude in a black city more terrible than any of the engravings I had seen of it. London was a city of suicides. And in France and abroad it was understood that the English were almost supernaturally inclined by temperament and coerced by their Moloch cities and shroud of weather into self-murder; the living went about Isleworth enshrouded in the green glow of death, embroidered with worms. The living dead copulated on Twickenham Road. The radiance of All Saints Church drove men and women into madness. If there was one place to chance to catch the sickness, it was here. The germ of my death was there, and in the struggle to comprehend the simultaneity that made this skull a place of many skulls.

My seminary position was the same as it had been at Ramsgate. My sermons were for dozens of boys who would otherwise smoke, drink, and masturbate through their puberty. I read them Blake's *Samson* and tried to make them afraid, but it was I who was afraid. When I looked into the boys' eyes, there was reflected the glitter of whores rolling in Judea like sparks on blue Galilee. In the confused whorls of my brain, as Vincent van Gogh, I knew that I was powerless in the face of primal sins. There was another in my head, another swinging from a tree in the sunlight, his intestines flooding a red desert. My nerves formed into a bright bouquet in my chest and threatened a vomit of flowers whenever I thought of the hypocrisy I felt trying to force virtue into these boys. The words were weak and not my own. At night, I shivered beneath a black woolen blanket and struggled to read by candlelight. There I devoured Dante and Milton and found myself to be jealous of the engravings of Gustave Doré, particularly of beautiful *Lucifer the Morning Star*.

Little Big Horn, June 25, 1876. That same night, in London as Vincent, I dreamed of a man named George Armstrong Custer. The Indians called him Son of the Morning Star. Custer was known for his long hair that shone red and scented with cinnamon oil. Vincent saw their faces overlap, his own and Custer's, for now on the day of his doom, Custer's hair was short.

The Cheyenne had sent their suicide boys Little Whirlwind, Cut Belly, Closed Hand, and Noisy Walking into the skirmish line, and the soldiers had cut them down. The Lakota surrounded them like a wall of fire. All was chaos. What had happened to Major Reno and Captain Benteen? Had they betrayed him? Crazy Horse, Gall, and Sitting Bull were somewhere in the howling smoke, and Custer's last men were horrified beyond breath. They put pistols to their own horses' heads and made defenses from their boiling bodies. The sky screamed and poured. The earth exploded upward to meet it. Far away, in England, Vincent van Gogh twisted in his bedclothes, his heart pounding. Custer's right arm took a bullet, and he felt as though a swarm of wasps had filled the wound. White Bull called out in triumph. Pretty Bird, a woman with hair as deep as a starless night, went through the soldiers' bullets like a ghost, and scalps blew in the tattered wind. Twenty-eight of Custer's last men fled without their weapons toward a black gulch full of Bibles, lace, and flags. The Indians swarmed about him. Custer took his revolver in his left hand and probed for his heart beneath his tan jacket. He refused to die at the hands of the Indians and had saved a bullet for himself; this was one of the laws of the plains. The grass of the hill was greasy beneath his boots. For a moment, the war was gone, and he saw nothing but the empty fields.

"I wish I could pass away like this," he said.

Custer shot himself through the chest.

I awoke to my cold room at dawn.

A single star remained visible through the dirty window.

* * *

ONE YEAR later, on December 23, 1889, I suffered a fit in which I felt like a man swinging in a noose, kicking my legs, dancing and dying over a field. Exactly one year had passed, like the distance between me and the other Vincent, and my hanging self. Time is a machine.

Auvers, July 27, 1890. *"La tristesse durera toujours."* The sadness will last forever. I took my paints and shouldered my easel for my last stand. Whatever had entered me, possessed me, or occurred to me in England had finally surfaced like an image previously lost in a poem. I am my own Judas Iscariot. The field rippled. Vincent took his revolver in his left hand and probed for his heart beneath his tan jacket. A tear ran down his cheek as he thought of Paul Gauguin and the Indians.

For a moment, the war was gone, and he saw nothing but the empty fields. I am a rebel angel, he thought.

"I wish I could pass away like this," he said.

Vincent van Gogh shot himself through the chest.

JUDAS ISCARIOT AND GÉRARD DE NERVAL
AS ILLUSTRATED BY GUSTAVE DORÉ

1855. La rue de la Vieille Lanterne. My name is Gérard de Nerval. My lobster blushes and clacks on its leash as we take in the Jardin du Luxembourg, the crustacean dancing on its ribbon, tied to my wrist. I am for the color black, the subterranean, the tenebrous carpet of the sea, the tar inside the world, hashish, and fingers moving into wet soil, as they would into a bulbous skull found beside a rotten tree. I am also for nature, her luminous breasts and weird angels, for the moth, the millipede, and the peacock. Ah, here come some children to mock my lobster and me as we walk. I shoot them, run them through, and mutilate them with my brain. But, still they come, the snot faces. They are no angels. My lobster raises a dismissive claw, I think. That must have frightened them. Then, as we pass a strip of roses, a terrier barks at us, and a bureaucrat calls us filthy.

"My lobster is clean from the sea," I tell him. "Your dog contributes nothing to this garden but shit, piss, and noise. Its stinking asshole runs around your house, and you let it onto your sheets and upholstery. You call my lobster dirty? Your dog can only defecate on your shoes in devotion. My lobster informs me of the mysteries of the deep!"

Such are my miserable days.

* * *

MY NIGHTS are spent beneath a wheel of mad stars. But everything is black and white, and it is quite clear. That is how night is, if you look at it with the right eyes. Another occupies my body, my frame, and ooze: it is a snarling errant spirit, flapping spastic from the pages of a Bible. That spirit fell into me as though it had fallen from the sky, through a hangman's trap, smash! The coordinates of my body were the end of his rope, strap! And it brought with it a roulette of foreign memories. I push him down as though we are two drowning fishermen, and he is my leverage to the skiff. He looks at me through the near-black water of our struggle, his eyes bulbous yet full of pity and scorn. "You think that breathing will keep you alive?" I know that he has been dead for centuries, but he is alive in me. We are two voices, fighting to be heard. We are one chimera. We are without time. My lobster and I are going for one last look at the Hôtel de Lauzon. We used to call it Le Club de Hachichin, and I was its treasurer, on the island of Dr. Moreau, the name we had given to the Île Saint-Louis, after Jean-Jacques Moreau, about whom we disciples would convene, loosely, Baudelaire, Gautier, Delacroix, and myself, in a rich, gaseous whorehouse of the brain. A fragment of paper blows between the slabs and flowers of Père Lachaise: *Do not wait up for me this evening, for the night will be black and white.* I wrote a book of madness and poetry entitled *Les Chimères* and will have an urn upon a pillar. I remember my travels in Judea.

With my hair in copper coils, my skull is the pornography of electricians, my features indistinct as a stone in slow weather. My suit is charcoal black, and I stand upright in Judea like a lightning rod for flies, fish wafts, and barbarism. The wind cracks my face like a wafer. The sun is my face reflected in an empty chalice, or a sphinx. The Judas trees roll across the hill-sides, a net of blood and blossom. The sky is the blue of drugs, of sharp signs in smoke or crystal. Who will be my Mephis-topheles, my temptation? No, I am he, and Jesus is my Faust adoring my mirage. I point out golden cities to him. His eyes follow my arm, wrist, fingers, to an event at the edge of our sight, where I inform him of his dominion, which is only the small yellow house of his birth. I am essential to his definition in ways that he is not to mine.

He is my blind rabbit.

When, finally, I come to die it will be by hanging. I will hang from a grating with an apron string around my neck that I will say was the garter of the Queen of Sheba. The dancing girls stripped off their seamed nylon stockings and threw slingshot shapes, sending them slowly down to the desert floor like scented black angels. Legionnaires snatched at them and wiped them across their lips.

THE KISS OF JUDAS

Here is a drawing by Aubrey Beardsley entitled *The Kiss of Judas* from *Pall Mall Magazine*, July 1893. Jesus feels his feminine shoulders melting into the hard and prickly bark of the tree where he reclines like a prince, long-haired and beautiful. We are in languor. The tree whispers his old trade back into his flesh. His mother's voice is in the breeze. Yet, as I lie down with him, he hears neither.

His lips are wet and insipid. They are like spoiled fruit. He listens to the gently conceited echo of his Self as the wood folds like a fleece around his neck and back, and a dutiful sleep descends for him. His robes lap about him. All is peaceful with him. Aubrey Beardsley—since I have entered into ambiguity and anachronism—draws me as a child, or rather as a man deformed and shrunken, stunted in the banality of childhood, tilting my grotesque bald head at

Jesus' groin. At the same time as they seem to show us, these figures do not. The child in Beardsley's illustration is not me but my descendant, one of the "children of Judas," the atavistic traitors. Aubrey Beardsley died after twenty-five years of life, the same age as Jesus and I. The truth is that I had no children. Nothing gathers so well, or is as pregnant, as a lie. I become the opiates in Beardsley, the spatter of grease from the bacon pan as he finds breakfast, the tight knot in his black tie.

The buildings of the city of London flowed like a torrent of black oil toward the heavens, leaving only scuffed ankle-high white snow on the streets. As he walked, Aubrey Beardsley lifted his knees high and flicked the ice from his shoes with sharp motions of his toes. He gave the impression of a fussy pony trained to wear tight suits and to walk upright, fastidious and awkward, old manners impressed upon a raunchy recalcitrant brain. Rising, dressing, bathing—all were imposed upon him. To look into Aubrey Beardsley's eyes was to gaze into satanic India ink, a swirl of loins and poisoned wells curling down into the bowels of the planet. All of the sex words bleached out of the Scripture scrolled like a pale, near-invisible dragon around his balls, the lozenge of his perineum, and the dripping catacombs of his skin. What hair remained on his body after his toilet was merely a fine smoke, an opiate auburn-black. His wrist was his reputation, the eroticist with the sunken face illustrating coils of sperm and stiff gods. Because his desires were terrible and shivering as thin dogs in the London snow, his copulations were monstrous and ornate. He saw all human bonds as lethal and treacherous. The world was without sympathy and as violent as he could imagine.

The gaslight fell on him through the snow. Beardsley was a sissy and a coward. His character had remained inchoate and suspended in the slime of his childhood, where he was thrashed for his filthy drawings. "So cold I shall perish before the front door." The syringe in his coat pocket would freeze solid and be ruined before he could shoot it. Moments later, he was home. The black door to his house shone like a mausoleum of rook wings. The dogs, Gog and Magog, barked at either end of the street when he opened it, and the smell of flesh poured out. He took in the street once more, the occult layers of it shifting beneath the ice, the wrought iron, the gas flares, the serpent of cobbles, the Gethsemane of soot, the Golgotha of bloody corsets, the many veils of Hell. He slammed the door with a flourish of relief. "I am still young to have seen what I have seen." He climbed his unlit stairs. "Such fevers."

When Beardsley was thirteen, he had stolen in to see a spiritualist. She had laid cards upon the rotting straw of the mews where she had set up. He touched himself through the material of his trouser pockets and caught the flash in the woman's lips. She stood over the cards and lifted her skirt and petticoats. The spiritualist pissed on the cards until they began to curl. The first card that she turned over depicted the image of a goat, wandering in a blasted desert. "Ah, the Scapegoat," the woman said. The second card was the Hanged Man. Something shook and seemed to kick Beardsley in the stomach, and the first seed of his life squirmed into his underclothes. For a moment, he saw the twitching obscene feet of a suicide suspended over rosy dirt.

The spiritualist came closer to him, piss steam around her ankles, brass bells and gypsy things shifting with her steps. "You are an Outsider," she said. "You will be anathema."

"I want to be an artist."

"You will only be trash, but a kind of spectacular, significant trash. Everything that you are, everything that you do, will be sick and dirty."

Everything that the spiritualist suggested came true because she had suggested it to him. Thus formed the noose of solipsism from which he would never escape.

Now, he collapsed on his bed, balancing a port and lemon on his skinny chest. The walls of his room were covered with pornographic drawings, images from the Bible, and romances of Judaic dust, chivalric and warped children. "I was ruined before I ever slopped out of my mother's inkwell," he reminded himself. He shot up and tried to draw, quickly, before oblivion took him.

The following morning, he breakfasted with Wilde at the Pall Mall Club. The early drinkers fanned and coughed through clots of smoke, waiters limped, and kippers steamed on white plates. A stuffed monkey swung by its neck in the strange rigging above the bar, surrounded by jaundiced portraits and picaresque paintings of naval or hunting follies.

"Ugh, my eggs are cold, again," Beardsley complained.

"Oh, do calm down, Aubrey. You sound like an old prostitute. Here, look at this." Wilde gestured to an advertisement in the newspaper that lay between them on the table. Wilde read the headline aloud. "It says *Spiritualist Medium Will Summon Biblical Witnesses*. It says that this fellow relays the voices of characters from the New Testament."

"Not the Old Testament, though?"

"No. Too untidy, I suspect. But, according to this, he does Paul, Doubting Thomas, and a bevy of tax collectors and cripples."

"I wonder if he would do Judas Iscariot?"

"Aubrey, come, that would be too easy. After all, the Church has insisted on giving us all a little bit of Judas and, signally, the likes of you and me. The Gospels, dreary as they are, make it clear that Jesus was strictly on loan—he has come, been, and gone. Whereas, you and I recognize implicitly that Judas Iscariot is of no place, no time, no race, no planetary space. He is ubiquitous in our spirit and, therefore, is the only thing in the wretched book, beyond the fornications and brutish sacrifices, that is truly *ours*."

Beardsley eyed Wilde across the table, the arrogant flop of his hair and the tight purse of his lips. "Go on."

Wilde spoke solemnly. "To be an anachronism, to betray one's time and place, is the highest of all the arts."

"We are all the children of Judas."

Later.

"Oscar? Did I ever tell you about the time I tried to hang

myself?" As they exited the revolving door of the club into the freezing Soho streets, Beardsley let his fingers drift over the Irishman's flanks.

"You never did."

＊　＊　＊

AUBREY BEARDSLEY pulled his ratty fur collar closer around his throat:

"I once convinced myself—although now I recognize that this is common in a certain caste of young men—that the universe existed merely as an ornate embroidery about me, that I was its agent, its concentration, and its scapegoat, that all else had been created by God as symbols and ciphers to surround me. Each experience became a message. Each sight, sound, and conversation became a code for something else. I was the *only* object in God's creation that was not a phantom. And all these phantoms, eidolons, and angels existed about me for the singular purpose of examining me and of watching me examine myself under God's awful lens. Every flame, birth, conflagration, worm, city, imagining, *everything* was an artifice, a moral burlesque . . . fucking, vomiting, dying, and conspiring about Aubrey Beardsley, whose trajectory was that of an artist. And in that scapegoat theatre, Wilde, I despaired.

"So, I fastened a rope to the cistern above my lavatory and pushed my face through the noose. I drank and drank until I was certain to lose consciousness, slump and fall, hang myself there. But the pipe was rusted and broke away. The deluge from the cistern washed over me, and, wretched as I was, I did not manage to die. I just sat there in the sobering slosh of my toilet. Ironically, that may have been the final proof that the universe really is set about me, and my affairs, and that even you are merely a cipher for my tuition. Or, rather, as I deduced, God is full of shit."

"Amen. Aubrey, I am writing a new erotic play called *Salome*. In the play, Herod has John the Baptist imprisoned in a cistern. I want you to illustrate my play. Will you do it?"

Beardsley's blunt hairstyle dripped with tubercular sweats, and he fought to steady his fingers as he inked the stripping of Salome and the destruction of John the Baptist. If there was to be Scripture, it should be illustrated with decadence. For, if it was anything, it was decadent. He dreamed in black and white. He was afraid that he was going to die young.

JUDAS ISCARIOT AND SKULLHEAD

1922. According to the politely folded invoices of the Agence Générale du Suicide of the Boulevard Montparnasse and its principal director, Jacques Rigaut, suicide by hanging, the suicide of the impoverished, could be administered for five francs. Should additional rope be required, it could be purchased at a price of twenty francs for the initial meter, and five francs for each subsequent ten centimeters. Other variations on suicide à la mode could be obtained, from low-end drowning through poison, revolver, and electrocution to the luxurious perfumed death that perhaps Samson and John the Baptist discovered something of. The agency toiled to sustain the dignity of the suicide, to arrange forbidden burials, prevent vandalism, dilute hysteria, and minimize contagion. It was against contagion that Augustine, the Papacy, the Church, and the Apostles set my stolen image. The hypocritical religious councils of sixth-century

Europe, at Orleans, Braga, and beyond, denied us funeral rites
as the demonizing of my death gathered force with grotesques
in illuminated manuscripts, stone relief, tapestry, and death-
paint. The Agence Générale du Suicide agitated and advo-
cated on our behalf. The Dadaists and Surrealists, exhuming
the memory of Gérard de Nerval, elevated the discussion of
suicide in the newspapers of the Left Bank. Rigaut crossed
his scuffed shoes on the surface of his writing desk and ran his
nicotined fingers across his brow. Notions formed connections
behind his face, which was as handsome as a gleaming snow-
plow blade. He lowered his feet and began to write.

Skullhead, the mawkish savage youth described in Rigaut's
Un Brilliant Sujet (A Brilliant Subject/Individual), experienced
dislocated apparitions of himself as a side effect of experimen-
tation with time travel. At first, Skullhead's intention was
to compel as many iterations of himself upon space-time as
were necessary to seduce his mistress, who had abandoned
him seven years before. Inside the slick and pulsing egg that
was his time machine, Skullhead's audacity ran amok. He ven-
tured deeper into the past, threatening to bring anarchy to
the Book of Genesis. Skullhead experienced ancient Judea for
months before locating the young Jesus of Nazareth slum-
bering beneath a tree. Skullhead injected potassium cyanide
into Jesus' skinny arm. In Egypt, he disfigured Cleopatra,
attacking her nose with a pair of pliers, leaving her to resemble
a disintegrating sphinx until her suicide. His ubiquity caused
him to appear as a god, worshipped in South America in
bloody sacrificial rites and all across the heathen continents.
Eventually, Skullhead declared a universal law mandating

suicide for all attaining twenty years of age. At least three science fiction writers unwittingly plagiarized Skullhead in the twentieth century.

It was 1929. For five years, Jacques Rigaut had existed—as he says—"on the other side of the mirror," which is to say that his suicide had become inevitable. Jacques Rigaut had suicide in his blood and set his face into the wind of his destiny with something close to joy, like a mariner enraptured by brilliant chimeras of polar ice. In the drawing room of a house in Oyster Bay, on July 20, 1924, Rigaut rushed headlong at an expensive art deco mirror, his fury growing and mimicking him, until the sleek silver frame passed behind his vision like a noose. The mirror cracked against the wall with the sound of a discharging revolver. But, Rigaut sustained only a slight gash to his forehead and seemed to stagger slightly back into the room, across the clay-colored rugs, while the damaged mirror swung on its hangings, as a guillotine would. In truth, he had transcended the mirror and, like myself, entered into anachronism and ambiguity. From that moment on, he had passed beyond the mirror. Perhaps he was already dead. From that dispassionate vantage, he watched the world until, quite reasonably, he exhausted it.

Rigaut's most extensive work was called *Lord Patchogue*, and it concerned that life beyond the mirror. Here, again, we mirrored one another: his Lord Patchogue, like my Lord Jesus, was the lord of an imaginary kingdom. The bourgeois critic prefers art to be mimetic; to present a mirror to life; to mimic its routines, surfaces, and costumes. Artists like Jacques Rigaut or myself—those who have transcended the mirror—care for it only insofar as it may be used to ridicule and offend. Rigaut once said: "Try, if you can, to stop a man who travels with suicide in his buttonhole." And Rigaut's mission, his mock passion, was as suicidal as mine or that of Jesus, my brother. Once passion is set in motion, it cannot be apprehended.

Uncertain of meeting God and powerless to modify a past from which he himself was issued, Skullhead concentrates on creating new versions of himself which are just different enough to perplex those of his contemporaries who might subsequently venture back into the past only to find nothing there any longer that corresponded with their historical expectations. Toward the end of the reign of the Emperor Augustus, Skullhead, after roaming the province of Judea for six months, stumbles across a child who is Jesus of Nazareth asleep under an olive tree: he injects potassium cyanide into the child's veins.

November 6, 1929. The Clinic at Châtenay-Malabry is close to where Chateaubriand, writer, explorer, and lover of flesh, lived and died clutching his wooden crucifix. Jacques Rigaut wandered within the gardens of the clinic, bearing with him a valise containing the necessary tools of his trade. His arm ached from needle punctures at the crease of his elbow. The pain was familiar and as much a part of his experience now as the blinking of his eyes. The grass was wet, and sometimes the earth curled through it like minced meat. The floral beds were without color. A light rain was beginning to fall as he stood beneath one of the chestnut trees. In that moment, he thought of me, and my death, swaying gently and terribly from a bough, and of how Chateaubriand had, at first, experienced Judea with revulsion. Rigaut had not experienced revulsion in half a decade, at least.

He shook his valise, and his tools rattled inside. He opened it slightly, but so as not to let the rain inside, and retrieved his metal flask of cognac. His innards leapt magnetically toward it as he flipped the cap with his thumb and poured the contents into his throat. Then, he crossed the swollen lawn to the doors of the clinic where he had a room, idly discarding a pocketful of morphine syrettes from his soft coat pocket onto the grass, like a trail back to the tree where he imagined me—that is to say, Judas—hanging. He was admitted with familiarity. He walked the pale corridors to his room, noting the smell of medical alcohol all around him.

Rigaut appraised his room from behind the mirror, which was screwed to the wall above the washbasin. His valise was open on the bed, where he had pulled back the sheets. He had taken the precaution of fitting one of the rubber sheets that the clinic kept to the bed. He lay there, with a draughtsman's ruler held in his left hand, measuring the precise location of his heart. In his right hand, he held the revolver, which he had declared to be the only literature on his bedside table. The pillow with which he had intended to silence the discharge was obliterated and feathers fell through the room, sticking to the little scorched black vortex in his chest. It was as profound and beautiful a scene as he had ever witnessed. He had cleaned his teeth and nails several times, and his hair was shining and immaculate. The Ruler and the Revolver, the Revolver and the Ruler.

⋄　⋄　⋄

IN TRUTH, we envy the fierce clarity of the death note on the dashboard, the doubtless soliloquy on the leather uphol-stery, the wedding band in the ashtray, the rejection on the mantel. We are jealous of the end of deliberation; God is in his prison amid the cinders of an immolated bush, dragged back down into the roots and soil of fear and imagination. They are done with vanity and pride. The details are a board game: the Pop Star with the Rope in the Kitchen; the Poet with the Oven in the Kitchen; the Painter with the Razor in the Studio; Ian Curtis in the Tombs of Mancunia; Sylvia Plath sniffing out Lazarus in London; Mark Rothko's armpits filling with blood on the Painting Floor of New York. The prepara-tions and artifacts, the milk and bread set out; the rubber sheet spread across the bed; the ruler to measure the distance to the heart; I am the shadow that swings out over all of these.

LADY LAZARUS, A SELF-PORTRAIT

In the gnarls and pits of Bethany, we first encountered Lazarus. When I was still young, I had a job in Bethany as a peanut seller. Bethany was close to Jerusalem on one of the southerly slopes of the Mount of Olives. Mary Magdalene would return to her home there after a night's whoring. I would meet her in the lamplight in a miasma of oil and the perfumes of sex, and she would disclose what she had learned of the scandals and events of the following day; if there was to be a crucifixion, a stoning, the assassination of a Roman soldier by guerrilla fighters, Mary would know of it, and I could be at hand to earn my money.

Lazarus as painted by Vincent van Gogh from the sanatorium at Saint Rémy in 1890, a moribund redhead propped upon his elbows as his sister Martha screams outside the tomb and I, Judas, look on; Lazarus is played by Vincent van Gogh. It is a self-portrait. Lazarus was subject to epilepsy, worsened by periods of hunger strike against the Occupation and a hysterical imagination. He would take to his bed for weeks at a time, starving, febrile, and tormented by paranoia. It was here that we would rehearse the miracle that Jesus would administer ten years later.

"Do you know the red-haired painter, the queer fox-face that lives here in Bethany?" Mary Magdalene asked me as she took peanuts from my bag in the insect-filled night.

Vincent stared at the window from his sickbed, watching his reflection and the lampshade that was the color of skin reclaimed by a factory. One fraction of his skull told him to rise from his cot, but his nerves and muscles would not obey him.

Lazarus did not fear his sickness itself; he had come to understand it as a mode of catharsis. A violent pressure would generate within him and finally explode, sending him into spastic convulsions and an oblivion that was kin to death. It was darkness with lightning storms and luminous worms, distant voices that spoke poetry like women, and a quiet shivering of orgasm. Slowly, he would arise, red as a phoenix, the taste of his decay on his lips. He knew that there would be one convulsion from which he would not return, and he had spoken of it to his sisters Martha and Mary. It seemed that it had come. Lazarus lay in the blank of his extinction, listening to the eerie silence of his cave. One fraction of his skull told him to rise from his pallet, but his nerves and muscles would not obey him.

I arrived at the home of Lazarus, Martha, and Mary with my bags of peanuts. As the whore had predicted, a small crowd had gathered, expecting the death of their neighbor; there were few examples of sorrow but much spite and relief.

A tax collector named Matthew said: "Martha is crying wolf again."

"No, this time I think he'll die." Bartholomew picked at his skin, and then he cupped his hands at his mouth to be heard shouting into the house. "Just kill yourself, Lazarus, and be done!"

Dreadful birds hung in the trees.

Before noon, I did excellent business.

"But he does this all the time," a cynical Pharisee complained. "His constitution is petrified. The only things he does not fear are these blackouts. Lazarus is weak and believes himself entitled. He calls himself an artist and so believes that God should exempt him from hard work, taxes, and engagements with reality. Here, I'll take some peanuts, boy." I handed the Pharisee a small bag. "When God does not fulfill his wishes, Lazarus here throws fits, tantrums, retreats and pretends to die, only to begin afresh with his delusions. Lazarus is a self-murderer by means of his overweening self-pity." He stuffed a fistful of peanuts through his beard into his curled mouth and peered through the window to see the redhead corpsing in his sheets. "Bastard!"

Others cried out, also.

"Charlatan!"

"Coward!"

And I too: "Get up, Lazarus!"

Martha, her fists clenched above her head, screamed for silence.

And then Lazarus awoke.

His draped skeleton pushed itself onto its elbows, and he slowly pulled the white cloth from his brow.

"I have done it again," he said to himself.

Ten years later, Jesus and I would return.

LIVE AT THE WITCH TRIALS

Massachusetts. 1977. They remained like that for some time, the Sylvia doll and the Anne doll, silent as dumbbells strung on the transparent umbilicus of jealousy and desire that twitched between them across the dining table. They were like twins. I stood behind them in turn, lowering my nostrils into the oblivion of their hair, Sylvia still scented from her small Auschwitz, Anne retaining her scent of imploding racetracks. Sylvia cast me a glance that she did not want me to see, but in that glance Bibles wrecked on black Atlantic rocks like black dresses torn on broken cocktail glasses and ravens rolled in white, empty tombs. She hadn't even touched her sandwiches. I kissed Anne full on the mouth, even though she was only eighteen inches tall, and I knew it wasn't going to work.

The second time I meant to write it out. Anne and I lit matches and struggled with our memories to pick our way through a blacked-out city. We were in the part of the city where the trucks are vented for screaming animals. But the city was still. We fought to hold the yellow glimpses we caught of it, like beer running through cupped hands. She handed me her cigarette as I slid my hand into her flank, pushing nylon into the exclamation mark of her ass. The dark was terrible. *This is how it is before you commit suicide*, she explained. *Everyone else appears to be dead before you. There is no light.*

We made our way inside the cocktail lounge of a hotel where dead people lolled against pianos, their bodies like splitting fruit, entire parties suspended in gas. We stole a bottle of gin and swam out into the street, climbing through the window of a parked car. Her glossy heels tore the headliner as I lay on top of her, spraying stars into her mouth. But Sylvia was missing. She stared at what I had written as though her eyelids were fanned with teeth.

Poets are more interesting than poetry. You probably think of me as blasphemous, and the truth is that I am not much of a reader. I do not like to read. Reading is like finishing someone else's painting. But a painting or a television will radiate into a room unbidden. There is nothing worse than the sneer of closed books. A book is a dead bird that you are expected to bury. I remember when Sylvia and I watched *From Here to Eternity* on television, and we lay down on the carpet in front of the scrolling metallic waves that flashed over Burt Lancaster and Deborah Kerr as they rolled on the beach; we were their mirror. She pulled my cock out and milked it all over her tweed skirt, her blouse open over one raging fuchsia nipple, and her skin subterranean pale beneath the coal mist of her stockings. She was something I had pulled from beneath the earth. The wind blew in from the white-hearted water. Anne thrashed at a typewriter in the next room, a firing squad of words.

It seems so distant from me now. But I do remember. They disintegrated in their quiet way, the way dolls will, without hysteria. I became ashamed of playing with suicides, waiting for the dolls to act while I was out of the room. I once put a wine glass outside on the window ledge of my apartment, above the street. It stayed there for a long time, as I would go out on my errands, and otherwise turn my back on it. I knew one day it would fall, and perhaps it would fall and do great damage, raining viciously into a baby carriage, or, perhaps, it would fall on me, the stem protruding from my brow beside the hot dog stand. Eventually, I brought the glass back in from the ledge. I wanted awful things to happen to people or, rather, to me. Nothing ever did. I never got caught fucking my poet dolls. I was never fired from work for masturbating with them in the ladies' room. I lived in my mind, like you do, in Smith College or Glenside Hospital.

❖   ❖   ❖

BROOKLYN. 1977. Inside the perfumed coat, in the shadow cast by mannerisms and mode, under the fur collar, behind the monocle of shilling gin, I negotiated the snowy barbarism of the city. I was nothing more than a stem of glass, transparent, hollow, and skinny. The city threatened me because he was a narcissist, a flower blooming in frosted black tar. I waited in restaurants like Lucifer in a church, goosing boys and sucking paté from my fingers. Fear perforated my lungs. My coat pockets were plump with my latest sex drawings, and my hair betrayed me. My hair was awful because I was an artist. I carried little flesh, just angles and bone. My eyes faced inward, showing their backs, mother-of-pearl, a few coils of gore and a flash of blue. Because I was an artist, no one ever saw my eyes. Because I was a coward, involuntarily I closed my eyelids when I spoke.

JUDAS ISCARIOT, SALOME, AND THE DECLINE AND BETRAYAL OF JOHN THE BAPTIST

As Salome, I was a clutch of caprice and spite. Within the span of those years, I betrayed my friend the Baptist, John, who was also our blueprint for messianism, eschatology, and the single-minded pursuit of one's own death. In those days, the Baptist was imprisoned. My father, that was Herod Antipas, held him in a cess tank below our grandiose palace. The cess tank and the labyrinth of pipes echoed with the prisoner's obscure nasal songs, like the plumbing of the Manchester Free Trade Hall where the sleet had been in my hair. The way he sang kept the stink out of his nose. Herod liked the Baptist, but my mother, that was Herodias, loathed and feared him, as though he were a tarantula.

The palace of Herod Antipas was a place of flesh, and the walls were embedded with lost hubcaps, jeweled lobsters, and blue and white latrine tiles. It pulsed to a slow rhythm as Herod would heave and ooze his fat body down its halls. It was as though the massive structure were masturbating. Herod had bowel cancer, and his finger would idly return to his anus, drifting up his glittering skirts; he was like a child discovering his smell for the first time. A white parrot sat always upon his sunburnt shoulders, preening demonic advices and increasing Herod's appetites, or so his wife believed. One of his appetites was for me, Salome.

I cast myself in the figure drawn by Aubrey Beardsley and dictated by Oscar Wilde. I was as ripe as my father's cancer, a beautiful bleeding star, part delicate china and part machine gun. Dressed in my peacock skirt, I made my way down to the cistern to see John. He was chained to a pipe in the gloom.

"My sweet Iokanaan, precious John, you know you could be released if only you swore to stop the baptisms and calls for the end of the universe."

John had deteriorated. The lightless prison had infected his skin with pallor. The girth of his thighs had diminished, and the broad, definite shafts of his muscles had turned to thin threads of milk. Some distant hand had rendered him down. John was fading and vulnerable, like Samson. His hair was lank on his shoulders. His eyes were all but emptied of the bright promise that had drawn men and women to his baptisms. All about us, the prison was without color. The swelling of the river had been replaced by the tedious dripping of the cistern.

Anxiety and arousal were drawn in monochrome whorls. Even the voice of John the Baptist had receded and came like a weak echo from a shell.

"I am a dissident," he sighed. "I sing dissent, but I am only part of a mechanism, like a part of your father's latrines. I serve no other function than to presage the coming of the mightiest, the father of all orphans, the probing lightning and the sun and the moon."

"The moon is furious tonight. Do you see her? She stands close at hand, here." Slowly, I peeled the corset from my breasts.

"I will not look at you, monster." His blood quickened.

"I am snow; there is dew beneath my peacock skirts."

"Take your poisonous eyes away from me. Look away from me, harlot." John's eyes were subterranean black, absolute.

"But you will regard me. Your head will stare at me from a silver plate. Listen to that noise above, where the Jews are quarrelling over your prophecies. There are some gamblers who believe in you, but the others think you mad."

"Whore, you will not make me afraid. Look away from me."

"Would you rather be strangled? That is what happened to the last prisoner down here. My real father, Herod Philip, was throttled at the command of his brother Antipas before the tetrarch married my mother. A colossal Nubian garroted him until blood sprayed from his neck. I know that you condemn the marriage of Herod Antipas and my mother Herodias. In silence, I would do the same. Can you not be your own conscience, rather than seeking to be the conscience of Jerusalem and the entire world?"

The Baptist's voice grew tender. "Salome, daughter of death, you are living on the edge of a knife yourself. With a sweep of his palm, the mighty one who comes after me will declare the end, the *end*, of all myths and the supremacy of one estate. The false gods of dirt, blood, oceans, and storms shall be obliterated; Zeus, Tiamat, Quetzalcoatl, Ra, and with them Shiva, Thor, Pan, and the rutting lesser gods, and with them, the lies of centaurs, hermaphrodites, sphinx, and nymphs, Minotaur and djinn and magic will be benighted. He will work miracles, but all else will be death."

"I hear my mother Herodias calling for me."

"Then good. Be gone."

"Does the fever of your arrogance ever let you sleep, John?"

He did not answer me, but rested his cheek upon the wall that echoed like a metal ship with the sounds of the palace of Herod.

My parents, as I will call them, subsisted in a perpetual state of drunkenness and were dictated to by violent whims. Sometimes, Herodias would storm into my bedroom and tear down my posters of punk rock bands. Herod would steal my underwear from the steamy laundry and jerk off with it. My body was the battleground where they would fight out their next divorce. Only an evil man or a capitalist will tell his own daughter that she should become a stripper.

"How do you obtain what you desire?" Herod inquired of me.

"By performing that which you least desire," I said.

"By prostration, sacrifice, compromise, and humiliation?"

"Heaven's gates are oiled with abasement and abjection," I explained.

"Does the prisoner, this Baptist, tell you this?" Herod's lips curled into an envious snarl, full of the erotic violence he intended toward all of us.

"He has his head in the lion's mouth, and he begs you to bite."

"Ah, well, I will not. Now tell me, Salome, daughter, what do you most desire from my glistering estate?"

"I would have the Baptist's head on a plate of silver."

"That is too much!"

"Really? Too much, you say?" I shook my shoulders, and my breasts shivered beneath the argent gauze of my shift.

"Perhaps . . ."

I stripped away my seven veils, and they fell to the floor in the smoky applause of Greenwich Village. Cigarettes dangled from terrified lips as I held the severed head in my hands and kissed the dead lips, pushing my tongue inside the surreal skull, as I would in Gethsemane. Men bought me drinks and gave me money because I was a traitor to my sex.

I was the female Judas.

THE TERMINAL RACETRACK:
JUDAS FINDS PILATE IN THE BELLY
OF THE BEAST

Judecca: the terminal racetrack. Hell spiraled down in concentric circles and walls of death. I pulled down my goggles against the phosphorous snow drifting against the spires of ice that rose out of the gashed floor. A dying sperm whale gaped on the plateau, hollowed out by terrible birds. The tail had been torn away, turning the creature into a vile funnel that still connected two shelves of ice across a black ravine. The creature made no sound, but a dismal fountain of gore piped from its blowhole. Ravens dipped their beaks into it and pulled off sheets of skin. The only way to cross the ravine was to walk through the innards of the whale. I ignited a flare from my pack and stepped into the creature's mouth. Silver sparks and smoke filled the cavity and then receded and gave a less blinding light. From farther inside the whale, I heard a man whimpering. I strode into the belly of the beast. When I discovered him, the man was wiping his hands against the flesh walls of the tunnel as though it could make them clean; instead they became more slathered in blood.

"Please, give me something. Help me rid my hands of this blood."

"Pilate."

"Is that Judas that was once my page?"

"The same."

"But grown! Oh, marvelous boy, surely you can help me. This is the whale Doubt who spans the ravine. This confinement is one of my punishments."

"But you are not confined, Pilate. Both the mouth and the tail are open to either side of the ravine. This belly sags over the abyss and will probably fall, in time."

"I could walk out of the mouth, yes, but the birds would come down for the blood on my hands, and they would rip my fingers and knuckles from my palms. Tell me what I should do! No, that is why I am here. I abdicated and a man was scourged and crucified."

"I sent him to you, Pilate."

I recalled the manner in which I became page to Pontius Pilate.

The fishing skiff that I had stolen to escape the island of Korkyra, after the accidental hanging of the aristocrats' girl, came aground on a sandbar, and seeing only a malnourished and sea-wrecked child aboard, a Roman soldier waded out to rescue me. The stink and shape of the skiff were like a ruined whale. The mast had sheared off in a black storm, and the sail had howled away into the night like a ghost. The soldier saw that my eyes were bare slits, like a goat's eyes, and that my skin was burnt and cracking and my red hair knotted and wild from the sea. His armor flashed in the scarlet dawn, and when I tried to speak, flecks of salt powdered from my lips. Gulls poured out of the sky to fight over the fish scraps littering the bottom of the boat. My cheek fell against his breastplate as he bore me back to the shores of Judea. His purple-red skirt shifted like the tendrils of a jellyfish. I drifted in and out of consciousness, glimpsing my mother Cyborea in a stable stall, laying out tarot cards and urinating on them; I saw a guillotine falling upon the neck of a man I recognized; I saw a goat staggering in the blooded soil of an alien planet; I saw the whole world bewitched by the image of a young prince contemplating suicide on a stage.

In those days, Pontius Pilate was stationed on the coast. It was to his mansion I was taken by the man who plucked me from a reeking skiff on the sandbar.

"Malchus, loyal Malchus, you have brought me a drowned fox," Pilate said to his slave. I had been mistaken in my delirium, and the man was not a soldier, but he did wear the livery of Pilate's retinue.

"My lord, I found him washed aground, alone in a fishing boat."

"Alone, you say?"

"He must have been at sea for weeks. The skiff was named *Corcyra*, and from its decoration, I think it must have come from there."

"Corcyra. That name reminds me of Cocytus, river of wailing, deep in Hell. Fetch water for the boy, and let us hear what he might have to say." Pilate put his hand to my brow and pushed the hair from my eyes. I remember that he made a show of needing to scratch his nose, suddenly curious of the scent on his fingers, in the same sly manner in which I had seen Herod sniff at his fingernails. "And I must wash my hands, also," he whispered. "He smells like fish and carrion." The slave Malchus laid me out on a divan. With the water, he brought aloe and treated my sunburn. Days later, when I had recovered a little and had managed to eat without vomiting, I sat with Pilate on his balcony above the vineyard.

"I want to keep you here, Judas," he said.

"I have nowhere else to go."

"I will employ you, as I do Malchus. I can retain you here at my home, and Malchus can return to the vital business of listening."

"Listening to what?" I asked.

"Malchus has very sensitive hearing. He heard you crying in your boat before he rescued you. Dressed as a native, disguised, he moves freely among people and listens to their plots against us, their gossip, and their vendettas and morale. His ears keep my territory safe. I probably know more of the petty intrigues and affairs of this place than any housewife, whore, or innkeeper." Pilate's smile was bright.

"Malchus is a spy?"

"If you like." Pilate handed me a small plate with bread and goat butter and a glass of red wine. He was relaxed in my company because he assumed that I had come from across the sea and knew nothing of Judea. "Now, Judas, my drowned fox, you can work for me, also. But we will brook no intrigue. You will become my page, which means that you can bring my wine, arrange my clothes, and so on. I awake frequently in the nights and will often require you to bring me wine, then to help me sleep again. Do you ever have dreams, nightmares?"

"All the time, my lord."

"As do I. As a matter of fact, you were attendant in a dream of mine last night. I dreamed that we had been promoted. Jerusalem was my station."

"A premonition!"

"Let us hope not."

"But why?"

"That is merely part of my dream. For the rest, I had crucified a man, a pathetic, innocent man, and two other criminals were with him upon the hill Golgotha, the place of skulls. As the evening came, so did a terrible storm. It rained so heavily that the ground became infirm, and the cross of the innocent man began to lose its foundation. It came down, slow and terrible as the mast of a sinking ship, until the man was being splashed by the bloodstained mud that had been far beneath him, now only inches from his face. And he was not yet dead. In the ghastly moonlight of my dream, eleven comrades of the innocent man pulled the spikes from his broken wrists and feet and stole him off the cross. The man came to my quarters like a ghost, and he opened his mouth, gaping and awful as though he had risen out of a tomb. His breath was a million deaths, and from his open mouth a sword blade extended that pierced me through my heart, as I lay paralyzed in my bed. You stood beside him, the twelfth comrade, Judas, with the keys to my palace."

"That is not possible, my lord!" I lied because I wanted to belong, but since my mother Cyborea had been a spiritualist, I recognized that Pilate's dream was the patina that embellished the mere truth.

"That is why I must keep you close."

I wanted to belong.

Weeks passed before Malchus approached me in one of the tiled corridors of the mansion. His whispers hissed furiously as he dragged me by the hair into an antechamber. "To think that I dragged you from the course of your death!" He clamped his hand over my mouth, as I was about to scream. "There is *talk*," he said. "There is talk, and there are stories of a boy who raped the daughter of aristocrats on the island of Korkyra and fled in a stolen fishing boat after the girl hanged herself in shame. The little rapist was a fox-faced bastard, like you. What do you say, Judas? Is this you?"

"No! I did not rape her! We were in love, but she fell from a tree where we were hiding and caught her neck in vines . . ."

"Liar." Malchus pushed his fist into my chest, and I fell back against a tapestry. It fell upon me, like the sail of the skiff had done in the night wrap of the storms. In my rage, I hurled it into the slave spy's face and punched at him while he could not see. I bit at his exposed cheek and sank my teeth into his ear. I kicked his groin and ran for the door. I climbed the mansion walls in panic, slashing my hands on the spikes of glass, as Malchus swashed through the vineyard with his sword. On the island of Corfu, at Easter, they still smash plates as though they are stoning me.

I would see neither Malchus nor Pilate for many years, until Pilate had received his promotion to Jerusalem, and Malchus would lose his wounded ear at Gethsemane. Pilate had a way of referring to Jerusalem. He called it *axis mundi,* by which he meant that it was a confusion of worlds.

THE DMZ

Recall the sand careening through the white hooded streets, a storm of sharp teeth and posthuman music, capsule monkeys incinerated in falling orbits, hookahs erupting, and writers drinking ash in the DMZ. I had heard they were serving duck livers at the Etemenanki Hotel that afternoon, the hotel where I had first met Conrad Eberhardt in its purple tiled foyer. Now, I found him asleep on a black damask chaise longue, a damp newspaper tented across his face. He was using it as a bug filter. His suit, like mine, was streaked with work. Eberhardt had described himself to me, when we first met a year ago, as "an orphan of both the fascismas and the judaicos, once of a wealthy family, then the child of Europe, and now, utterly deracinated except for the verdigris of my name and my passport." He pulled the newspaper from his face and rolled onto his elbows, appearing somehow, despite the conditions, immaculate and dapper as a sphinx. His sandy hair was waxed at an angle from his brow, and his lips were pursed in an attitude of concentration of which I knew him to be incapable. Despite that, Conrad Eberhardt was the best writer in the city and, since none of us would ever get out, the world. I would try to imitate him. He reached into his jacket and retrieved a small round tin. "It's just the one tin, I'm afraid."

"Duck livers. Conrad, how on earth did you get them?"

"I picked them up near the airport, where the minefield begins, while I was covering that story on the photojournalist."

"Flynn?"

"Yes. They must have been dropped or ditched by smugglers, but there they were in the weeds beside my left shoe. At first, I thought it might be an APM, but then I could see the blue label on the side: Mesoamerican Duck Livers. So, I put my foot over it and stood there until all the drama was over, which, as you know by now, was considerable."

"How *long* did Flynn last?"

"He was very drunk. I would say he ran for about thirteen seconds shooting film constantly and screaming, straight out, into the minefield. His flashbulbs flared the whole place up, and we all cheered, for some reason. I think he took a small hit after about six seconds, but the mine was compromised and just sort of *nibbled* at him like a piranha, rather unlike the last one, which took his legs clean off. Pieces of him showered down on us for several seconds, a kind of cannibal confetti. It was ironic, me standing there with my foot on the shiny tin. Shall we have them now? I'll get them cooked up. *Yallah!*"

Eberhardt clapped his hands together, and a pale Etonite

child in a batik shirt scuttled out from behind the violet drapes and made off with the tin like a ball boy in tennis. Moments later, we were sitting together around a small Bunsen burner as the livers fried in a black pan, sharp organ smoke leaking into the room, until Eberhardt raised his finger and the boy switched off the gas lung and retired. "He won't tell anyone." The boy set off a flower bomb in the foyer: pink smoke and roses.

"He doesn't want this place closed down," I suggested.

"Neither do we." He raised his tumbler of coffee and I raised mine.

"Hear, hear."

We were both entirely apolitical, an orientation made necessary and easy to maintain by the fact that politics had ceased to exist; all that remained were the Tiresian games of government: the exchange, every seven years, of sissies for toughs, hawks for doves, that passed for progress in the DMZ. The Etemenanki Hotel was our underground, our safe place of the spirit. Eberhardt explained about the duck livers. "These livers contain a toxin closely related to dimethyltryptamine. These South American ducks squeeze the poison from the glands of toads with their beaks. Some years ago, a series of Mayan or Olmec—I don't remember which—relief works was unearthed, and they showed these Mayans wearing duck masks and worshipping these birds because they could ingest the toad poison safely, and, well, their livers became reservoirs of hallucinogens. In a few moments, you and I could be *anywhere.*"

A gelatinous spectral fist took my intestines, crushed them, and flung them toward the street. They hung like seaweed in the revolving doors and spattered the shins of a camel. Another hand pressed upward from beneath my chin and forced me through the ornate ceiling into one of the red rooms of the hotel. Eberhardt witnessed my distress. "None of this is really happening," he insisted. I stared back at him with my eyes turning black. I knew that he was right. It was one of the contraindications of expatriation, absence from the world, disinterest, and abstraction. My heart shook from its vessels and floated somewhere. "Let's get outside."

We regarded the flickering whites of eyes in the amorphous shifting of the black burkas outside, thick kohl sending strange hexes and admonitions, as though deadly fish swam into our air from another universe, piercing the clear membranes of time and space. The Olmec boy who trailed beside us through the market opened his mouth, baring one hundred tiny teeth and laughing like a can opener. He wore a piece of jade around his neck that was fashioned like a duck's bill. Soon, the sun would set, and the women would be compelled indoors. The dark was strange and masculine in a way that darkness had never been in Europe, voided. There were only café tables, detuned radios, tarot cards, magazines, small thefts, a cruel sinless boredom. Our hearts beat violently as we struggled toward the abandoned airport. We limped between the hangers and the dying candles of the runway. Searchlights tracked across the minefield. We clambered into a fire-gutted DC-10 and tried to fall asleep.

We were in the jungle. Emerald fronds fell over our eyes as we shielded our mouths from insects. Mist shrouded and ran us over. Eberhardt, naked and slimed with mud, hacked forward with his machete. We were climbing a sinus of flowers and filth. Leeches dripped from every surface. Rays of light dialed in from a sky that we could not see. The plane lay behind us, thousands of feet down on the jungle floor, smoldering in the seething earth, snakes and contorted foliage. Finally, we broke the canopy and found ourselves on the open mesa before the ziggurat. In moments, we were engulfed. Yet, for a few terrible seconds, it was as though we had entered a kind of vacuum, and no sound reached us from the appalling ceremonies that we witnessed. The fine back of Eberhardt's hand touched mine. "It's not real, of course." Then, the silence broke with an obscene gnashing of agonies and awe. It was as though every *National Geographic* image of Mesoamerica, every film set, every tourist photograph from a chartered helicopter, every single representation had been dragged through a developing tray of blood and coated with feathers. Blood flowed from the steps as thousands of ducks were torn apart, heads twisted off, wings rent and scattered into the desperate, joyous thrall of the crowd. The ziggurat was covered in gore and down, and the people, some of whom wore bird masks and crude wings, hurried from place to place, searching for organ meat, crouching, or prostrating themselves in visionary seizures. The brown confetti of feathers blown from the bodies of ruined birds clung to our bodies. Eyes began to fix upon us. Suddenly, we were taken. Eberhardt was thrown face down across a green slab of stone and bound to it. The people at the temple used jade utensils to scoop from the livers and carnage. The Olmec boy who trailed beside us through the market opened his mouth, baring one hundred tiny teeth and laughing like a can opener. He wore a piece of jade around his neck that was fashioned like a duck's bill. He chewed like a machine through Eberhardt's flesh until he reached his liver. With his duck's bill spoon he began to eat, pushing it into the flowing cavity, a tiny piranha moving into a current of blood. The moon rose and fell, illuminating the endless ceremony of duck, man, ziggurat.

When I awoke, Eberhardt was beside me in the charred cockpit of the DC-10; the sun rose over the minefield before us and glazed the dewy runway and the dripping barbed wire. A thin crust of vomit surrounded his lifeless lips and his eyes stared directly into the sun, registering nothing. I clambered out of the plane, leaving him there, and wandered back toward the Etemenanki. I would take his room. We had sought the Promethean in the bars, hotels, pits, deserts, and jungles of the mind and it had killed him; we had grasped at the cold flame of our anonymity, stolen ourselves back from religions, states, and territories, but we were still afraid of the terrible mysteries that surrounded us or fell from the pages of magazines or glowed from newsreels. I have thought about it many times. There are things that I know beyond doubt. The languid expatriatism that belonged to the twenties and thirties had melted away, and I sensed in that which had been, a terror that had been subdued and concealed beneath the shades and that lingered with us still. It was a kind of failure, the notion that fear was everywhere and that no amount of coffee, cigarettes, or morning alcohol had removed the anxiety. The perfume of the flower bomb remained in the foyer of the hotel. The elevator was broken, and so I climbed the marble stairs to what would be my room.

Betrayal without end, the sacrifice of friends.

THE ACTORS PREPARE

The schism between guise and reality, between the actor and his prosaic life away from the conventions of drama, generates his sense of the absurd, and so the challenge of despair and death versus life. Albert Camus, who finally went by automobile when he should have gone by locomotive, was another who asked whether suicide was the appropriate response to absurdity. Despite my arguments nagging in his skull, the ineffable wisp of me in his Gitanes smoke, his own doubts as his pomade dampened his pillow, and my invisible jostling at the railway ticket office, Camus crashed on the wrong side of the question. *Au contraire, Sisyphus, Prometheus, Lucifer! Grin and bear it!* said Camus. The idiot.

Jesus of Nazareth lived with his parents, Mary and Joseph, in a shitty house in Bethany, on the slopes of the Mount of Olives, close to the city wall of Jerusalem. The whore, Mary

Magdalene, who was our age and our friend, lived nearby. It was a two-room dwelling, with one of the rooms sacrificed to Joseph's carpentry workshop, and the other room was kitchen, bedroom, and latrine, all in one space. The odors of sweat and shaved wood became indistinguishable. Joseph made crosses for the Roman garrison to crucify the seditious, the criminal, and the awkward. Jesus' father may have been the only man in Judea to loathe himself as profoundly as I did myself. He suspected the infidelity of his wife and the illegitimacy of his son. He was emasculated physically and politically.

One night, when I called upon Jesus at their home, I saw Joseph in his workshop, toiling over something, holding it briefly in the candlelight, but secretive and guilty. I knew that this was one of the rare times when Joseph created something for himself, alone in the blue-black shadows, when no one came calling for the apparatus of torture and death that sustained his family. I pressed myself into the gloom beside the doorframe and tried to observe him. I heard his knife scraping away at the wood, but my eyes could not adjust to the candlelight, and his great fists obscured his work. Then, fleetingly, I saw the misshapen features on its convex surface. Jesus' father was fashioning theatre masks for the city's Roman actors. I had seen them many times. The actors arranged themselves and hustled against the Western Wall of the city in the shadow of the hull of the dislocated ship that projected from the stones. There, they practiced their riffs, cons, and impersonations. In years to come they might act the plays of suicidal Seneca. But, in the hierarchies of the Occupation, their position was aligned with the petty criminal and the prostitute and was almost as dangerous. Their wooden carnival masks concealed the blooms of violence on their faces, where stones had been thrown at their performances. Such were the risks and injuries accumulated with assuming false identities, of being another.

Jesus' hand fell upon my shoulder, and he tried to drag me from the house. The shadow of the latest mask poured black over the yellow-lit ceiling as Joseph moved to test it against his own face. It was the mask of a tragedian with sculpted tears, curled lips issuing a terrible violence and revenge against the world that had destroyed him. Despite being a pariah to the meaningless men and women of Bethany, Jesus' father was pleased to make crosses for the Roman Empire; there was a chance that he might make the instrument of the death of his wife's lover. It sickened him to pretend that the boy Jesus was his son, to protect her, to maintain illusions, and to sustain hypocrisy. He would make an army of such masks and animate them in his darkest and most hopeful dreams. Jesus, I reasoned, must know that his father was an actor.

※　※　※

JESUS AND I walked to the city gates. A wedding party was continuing into the early hours of the morning. A tall, hairless eunuch with skin painted gold had lifted one of the bridesmaids so that her legs were spread around his shoulders; naked, he held her there with her back against the wall of the city while he licked and sucked upon her sex. The bridesmaid held her arms out like a cross against the wall and let her orgasm pump into the gold man's mouth. Another couple were dressed as angels. They removed their wings and lay them down on the sand. The bed of feathers slowly disintegrated as they fucked in the searchlights.

"I want that," I said, pointing at the lovers in the chaos of the Jerusalem DMZ. "To be a rebel angel, to behave as if rebelling against the universe were not just as facile as refusing to abide by illusions. I want the facts of my passion and my hatred to matter."

"My mother once told me that I was born because an angel visited her."

"At least she's not a spiritualist like mine pretends to be. Then again, my mother pretends intercourse with the supernatural too."

"Fuck yourself, Judas! Men are aroused by mentally disintegrating women; why should angels be any different?"

"You're right, Jesus. They probably prey on the weak and sexually frustrated. Well, idiot brother, for how long did you believe her?"

"I'm not certain that I have stopped believing her."

Jesus, even then, had a spectacular ability to superimpose absurdities, moral evasions, and wish fulfillment upon the landscape. He had an arrested desire to see another reality. He was frozen in that landscape, like a man in a painting. Disinterestedly, I provoked and experimented. Now, decades later, transfigured by my suicide, our suicidal mission, I have embarked toward a final confrontation on the frozen plateau of Judecca that bears my name, submerged in the winter of Hell.

That is how it began.

＊ ＊ ＊

WHEN WE were teenagers, it seemed that Jesus' heart was a black hole of solipsistic compassion, inexorably drawing the universe inside it with a romantic agony that is only so painfully experienced in adolescence. That scarlet beat of self-absorption, self-pity, and selfishness disguised as comprehension would pull everything inside its beautiful depression. First it would drag his left nipple across his breast, then his collarbone would dip toward it, and then his neck and chin would dowse for the hole, followed by his lips, teeth, eyes, skull; and when he succumbed, the junk of Jerusalem would be dragged in by a flash of appalling gravity, the Sea of Galilee would leap like a fish into him, and then the entire world; and all because he believed the force and depth of his passion could overwhelm all being. The ferocious blows of his sanctimony against the world would be too heavy for survival. Where I felt this as a cynic, he felt it as the Messiah. Yet, rather than trying to disabuse him of his feeling that the universe began and ended in his breast, I let him run with it, relentlessly and without restraint. Where we might have had other friends, we had only the whore Mary Magdalene. She seemed to be falling in love with Jesus, the only boy in Bethany who hadn't fucked her. When I screwed her, she would beg me to tell her more about the night when Jesus nearly drowned, when we visited John the Baptist, who had since been beheaded. "You gave him the kiss of life, Judas. Thank God that you put your breath into him! Let me put your lips on mine, so that I can feel as close to Jesus as you were the night when you saved his poor life."

"Sometimes, I wonder if I did the right thing." I kissed her, and our hips slapped together in the darkness of the alley.

"How could you say that?"

"Don't you see how seriously he takes his autonomy, now that he is old enough to stay out of the house, now that he has his affectations and feels that he can make changes to things?"

"It's good, Judas, it is *good*."

"No, you'll see. Autonomy for Jesus will mean despair for us."

"Please don't despair of him, Judas. Indulge him, if you must, be patient, and it will run its course. I know that the fantasy that I have of him, and that he has of himself, is just that." She heaved against me, her thighs shivering. "Let one lamb remain ignorant of this slaughterhouse for a while longer, *please*."

I know that she saw his face when I emptied myself into her.

I revisit this often, even against my will, particularly as I am crossing Judecca. It is all as known to me, as rehearsed and replayed as the soliloquy of Hamlet. The words and gestures come as though from machines. I stalk the galleries, witness the poles of our representation, paintings, engravings, stained-glass windows, haunt the wormy theatres, celluloid, listen to the whip crack of typewriters, both of us frozen: Jesus ascending from the boughs of his crucifixion, Judas descending from the limbs and noose of his suicide; Jesus' death the apotheosis, Judas' the nadir. These are the proofs of our fictionalization, the dramatic persuasion of death to prove a point, as gaudy, brutal, and stupid as an opera. How is the defeat of death known? It is not, unless you are I, journeying within the Plutonian cold of Hell.

It was Édouard Riou, a disciple of Gustave Doré, the great engraver of Dante's *Inferno* and of the suicidal hanging of Gérard de Nerval, who illustrated Jules Verne's *Journey to the Center of the Earth* in 1864. Vincent van Gogh and George Armstrong Custer shiver over their oil lamps, watching prehistoric monsters devouring one another in a fathomless subterranean sea.

STELLAR DEATHS IN MOTION

As Pontius Pilate had foreseen in his nightmare, Jesus and I were to gather eleven further disciples: Simon, who was also known as Cephas, whom Jesus called Peter, and his brother, Andrew, the fishermen; James and John, the sons of Zebedee, whom Mark called the sons of thunder; Philip; Matthew, the tax collector; Nathaniel, the son of Talemai; Thomas, who was also called Judas Thomas Didymus, the twin; James, the son of Alphaeus; Thaddeus, who was also called Jude and the son of James; and Simon the Zealot, who may or may not have been my father, according to the Gospel of John.

Jesus and I would walk the shores of Galilee, sharing a bottle of wine and watching the dawn stars fading as the fishermen went out. The last to disappear we called Lucifer, the morning star. Jesus was now taller than I, and his hair was as dark and lustrous as the moonlit sea. Sometimes, we would help the

fishermen haul their nets from their boats, but the wounds
in my hands from my escape from Pilate's mansion had never
healed properly, and they would bleed easily when I hauled
the salty rope; not so Jesus, whose wiry musculature concealed
a rude strength. The gloss of his beard caught the sun as he
laughed with Simon and Andrew, who were not yet our disciples.

"Pity poor Judas! Pilate had him half-crucified by mistake,
but he was cut down in time. He has the marks in his hands
and feet!" Jesus had a laugh that was as forceful as the roar of
a lion.

Things had changed.

"And a lifetime's whoring has made him weak and red-
headed," Jesus went on, and our friends laughed with him.

"Still," said Simon, "you would both be welcome to fish
with us tomorrow. Have you ever steered a fishing skiff,
Judas? I bet you would be a natural."

"I never did."

"But you'll come with us, friend?" Andrew asked.

I nodded.

"He will be seasick!" Jesus laughed at me again.

By this time, I was living on the streets, my mother having
succumbed to uremic poisoning, perishing in a yellow cloud
of acid that surrounded her death pallet, the paraphernalia of
her scams, tarot cards, voodoo dolls, scrying glass, and stained
Ouija board scattered about her as relics; and my father having
gone underground as a guerrilla fighter, refusing to acknowledge me when I would encounter him in the darkness of the
city, garroting wire hanging from his black leather belt and a

dagger covered in oxidized blood, like the corroded night in Italianate murder paintings. I did not grieve so much, since they were not my real parents. The shades of my real parents hung amorphous and tantalizing in my dreams.

I slept rough in the red light district of Jerusalem and was often overwrought with nostalgia born of suffering. Scripture is nostalgia, and Judea was addicted to it. Like the distant sound of looms, the sense of wool underfoot in a lightless room, or the slow curl of a hashish cloud, the people of the city and the wild lands around drew some ineffable comfort from it. The homes hummed with it, for it was a means of looking inward, away from the hard truth of the Occupation. Scripture promised them an altered state, a different order that was mysteriously withheld. It illustrated their yearning for the absolute by means of veiled revelations, like a striptease. Therefore, they were more compelled by its weaving motions. Through obscurity Scripture offered them certainty. It resembled the practice of life well enough yet also remained sufficiently detached and strange to make them envy its fantasies. Scripture is for those who ask why we live. This is not a serious question. With the passing of each day, there were more prohibitions and prescriptions. I saw people immobilized in the vortex of a sandstorm of laws, encircled by laws and more laws. And I wondered if the only way to manifest progress in them was to halt this endless scrawl and sprawl of Scripture. They were imprisoned by illusion and complicity. But, if I could take such a man and throw him back into the mechanism, if I could take Jesus and throw him into that loom, he might knot it and strangle its perpetual threads.

Now, I lived inside the echo chamber of his arrogance and had no other home. The dogs let me lie down with them, and some nights I would sleep with one and some the other. There were nights when the dogs would share their meat with me, or I might have starved.

Jesus still had his family home, although Joseph was weak and bedridden now. Decades of sawdust had shredded the lining of his lungs, and he breathed with great labor and regret. The workshop was no longer a part of their home, which meant that his mother and father had a separate room to sleep in. Jesus kept the abandoned workshop as his bedroom, while Mary and Joseph kept the room with the kitchen and latrine. Jesus' room retained the miasma of sweat and shavings, even though the tools and lumber had long since been sold to another local artisan. He managed to keep the room locked, and on the small, high windowsill was the wooden theatre mask that I had seen his father carving that night in our childhood. To regard us now, you might think that our fortunes had reversed, and where I had been his Virgil, I was now but the shadow to his blinding light, but you would be mistaken; Jesus' lamp was only as bright as Judas' oil. I threw grit at Jesus' bedroom window to awaken him, and we made our way to the shore where the fishermen were preparing for the morning's toil.

"These are *the blue hours*," I said, feeling the spectral chill of morning, with the sun still not risen, the atmosphere on the edge of disturbance, the pale gulls mute.

Simon and Andrew were at their skiff before us, with a breakfast of warm bread and goats' milk that they shared with us. The two fishermen looked very much alike, both with receding whorls of dark brown hair, powerful shoulders, and strong wrists from pulling in nets, except that Andrew had lost the sight in his right eye to a gull when he was a boy, and there was now only a torn milky anemone of an eyeball beneath the half-closed slit of his lids. Andrew was the more cavalier of the two, where Simon was cool as a stone and measured in his every gesture.

"Simon was worried," Andrew announced, brushing the sand from a piece of bread that he had dropped and retrieved. "He's like an old fishwife over you."

"Worried?" asked Jesus.

"Judas, I don't like the idea that we might make you sick. The water will doubtless be choppy when we get out." Simon looked out at the low, serrated waves.

"What's a little vomit between friends?" I pretended to heave at Jesus.

"That's the spirit!" said Andrew. "Come!"

We hauled the skiff over the shale and out into the Galilee shallows, clambering aboard as the freezing water reached our thighs. The sun began to rise but was obscured by oily clouds at the horizon. The fishermen raised their small triangular sail, and the dawn breeze took us creaking out into the deeper water.

"I have been meditating on the subject of the occupation of our lands by Rome," Jesus told us.

"Are you to become a zealot like Judas' father?" Andrew turned on his narrow wooden seat. "Strangle legionnaires in the dangerous quarters of Jerusalem?"

"That man is not my father."

"No, no. Listen to me, Simon, Andrew, and you also, Judas. The spread of men across the world is like ink dropping upon a cloth. The blots of ink spread and overlap, and some are lost within others."

"Are you saying that this is desirable?"

"It is *natural,*" Jesus said. "We should not resist. Rome, despite all sophistication and declarations of intent and Empire, is merely a dripping quill. It is not a mind, a strategy, or volition. The ink that is Rome will dry up, and more ink will fall upon it and subsume it. Rome is not even an animal; it is an abstraction."

"But what of us, here, now?"

"Rather, give yourself over to he who holds the quill. To God."

"God should be more careful with his ink!"

"Damn you, Judas." Simon was finally irritated. "It's an analogy."

"So what? You think that because an analogy can be imagined, that it has any currency in the world?"

"Judas is right, Simon," Andrew said. "You hate to rock the boat." He winked his ruined white eye.

We were held between vast beating black wings. It seemed that the storm had come from nowhere. We had not even had a chance to put out our nets. "Thank God that our nets are in; they would pull us under!" Simon called out as the wind began to shred the sail. "Get it down!" I grabbed the ropes, and blood seeped from my hands. "I have never seen the water so violent! Your blasphemy!" Simon cried in terror.

Jesus stood up in the boat, and Andrew called for him to sit down. I saw it at the same time that Jesus did: a sandbar just beyond the skiff's splintering rail, just a glimpse of pale sand before it was washed over with the tenebrous waves. With absolute calm on his face, meeting the eyes of the fishermen who huddled aghast and sickening in the prow, Jesus stepped from the boat into the rain and chaos that was like the beginning of the world. To Simon and Andrew, he seemed to have stepped upon the surface of the water.

"Do not be afraid," he told them, outstretching his arms, his soaking white shirt a dripping ghost in the vortex, his hair whipping about his face. "God is with you. He breathes through the salt sea and overwhelms it; he breathes through your best and most rotten nets; he breathes through this skiff, the bark of your survival; he breathes black across the sun and brilliance upon the moon, and he breathes placid daylight after thunderstorms; he breathes through the eyes of the fish you will catch; he breathes here, but he will not blow you down."

Simon called him Rabbi, and Andrew called him Master.

I remained silent.

Jesus waited for his moment and stepped back into the boat, where the fishermen wept and embraced him, forgetting the howling gale and the vicious sting of the rain, until the tempest passed us by, and we were left with glassy blue water. And a miracle.

We reclined beneath an olive tree in the chill Bethsaida night. Jesus pulled ropes of his long dark hair across his face, inhaling the scented halo of salt and grease that hung about him. The bull's eye Aldebaran blinked though eons of dust. The belt of Orion glowed half-exhausted by toil, hung about with the shawls of beasts and skulls of dragons. I recalled the way my mother would speak of the stars, how they were set in chain, and of how men and women were controlled by them. I did not believe her. "But," I told myself, "we have set our most stellar deaths in motion."

          ❋   ❋   ❋

THE FOLLOWING morning, in Bethany, our brows aching from alcohol, we circled the bazaar in search of goat meat and bread. The sun was fierce, and the fishwives and slaughterhouse children who were made to work passed out water as we hesitated at their stalls. A camel weighted down with sweating ziggurats of dynamite was driven through the narrow alleys by weeping children, each of whom wore a scarlet fez and beat the camel with a cane. The canes whistled in the hot wind, and the camel bellowed and spat thick saliva across a tray of insects. They were heading for the Etemenanki Hotel. After that, we went to see John the Baptist, and we sat beside the river and drank water from paper cones. Simon and Andrew the fishermen were there, and they sat close to us. John was standing in the river, as always. We watched him push the heads of men and women beneath the water, as we had watched him as children. I had not yet become Salome nor betrayed him with my striptease.

Jesus pointed out some Levites, parking their motorcycles across the shale. They were letting their engines cool when a cluster of priests approached them, gesturing urgently, as though the motorcycles were still kicked into noise. "They are gesturing at John," I told Jesus, from the side of my mouth. The Levites were a homeless gang who wore a golden star upon the back of their black leather jackets. I liked the Levites because they were rootless like myself. Mary Magdalene had introduced me to them. They had come to drink at the river. Their presence there made the people who had come to be baptized shirk away, quietly gathering their clothes and sandals, covering their faces from mute shame. Jesus became nervous, and I saw water tremble from the lips of his paper cup. It reminded me of the storm water overflowing the rim of our fishing boat as Simon and Andrew bailed and cried out. We remained, not deserting our brother John.

The priests brought the reluctant Levites over to the edge of the water, close to where John stood washing his sunburnt shoulders and where we sat watching him. The priests shielded themselves behind bikers. One of the priests whispered in the ear of one of the Levites. I knew the Levite as Nitzan, or Bud, which was his gang name. He pulled off his leather cap and unzipped his jacket, revealing a sweat-stained T-shirt.

"Who's your friend, Judas?" Bud asked, and I was about to answer him when John stood forward out of the river, scuffing the gravel with his naked feet.

"I can answer the priests directly," he said.

"Who are you?" one of the priests, an old man with a broken nose, demanded from behind the line of Levites. The priest was named Zeev.

"I know what you want, but I am not the Christ," John said.

The priest was indignant. "What then? Are *you* Elijah?" Two of the Levites, Dan and Gershon, wearily stood aside and let the old man with his prodding finger through to stand in front of the Baptist.

"No. I do not think that I am the prophet Elijah, old man. I am just another voice crying in the wilderness, making straight the way of the Lord, as the prophet Isaiah said."

"Judas," Bud addressed me, "the Pharisees want to know why your friend is baptizing our men and women if he is not the Christ, nor Elijah, nor the prophet." Bud the Levite and John the Baptist looked like a Tom of Finland cartoon.

"I'll tell you," said John. "I baptize these people with river water, but among you is one, whom you do not know, who comes after me." Unnoticed by the inquisition, John flashed an eye at Jesus, who froze as though a lightning bolt had penetrated him; his whole system stopped dead for that moment before he was able to lower his head to his cup again and slurp in panic for distraction. "He who comes after me, I am not worthy enough to untie one thong of his sandals."

"We will go back and inform the Pharisees, and Herod Antipas, the tetrarch, also." Zeev folded his arms petulantly.

"Hey, motherfucker." Bud grasped him by his shawl. "You didn't tell us this was a squealing trap." Bud shoved Zeev down onto the wet stones. The old man's head cracked upon the ground, and blood began to flow into the river. "Let's stomp this bastard!" Zeev is a name that means wolf, but when the pack of Levites fell upon him, he split apart like a beetle, his skin desiccating in the noon sun as his corpse flowed away and the Baptist watched, passive, as did Jesus, Simon, and Andrew, as though they believed the lies of my mother, that all men are doomed by the stars. My plans required such passive drones. The Levites washed their boots in the river and returned to their motorcycles; twelve yellow stars upon their twelve leather jackets, they roared away in a cloud of dirt and gasoline fumes. I was aroused by the violence.

John came over to the place where we were sitting, and he indicated Jesus. "Behold, the face of the Lamb of God, who strips sin from the world. It is he, my general, the man who goes before and after me, whom I saw in a dream. He alone is the reason that I came to mission with baptisms of water, to reveal my commander to Israel." I watched the currents of madness and arrogance swirling together between my brothers, John and Jesus, and I seized my chance to agitate.

I demanded of John: "What dream?"

"I witnessed the Spirit, incarnate as a dove, descend from Heaven, and I saw that it remained over him, although I did not know him well then. It happened when you pulled him from the river, Judas."

I complained. "A hawk, surely. A dove cannot hang over a man."

"A voice without a voice instructed me that he on whom you witnessed the dove descend and remain, this is he who will baptize with greater than water, with the Holy Spirit, and I have seen the bird above this man, our brother Jesus, the Nazarene." And the sun shone upon the water so that we were all nearly blinded, and Jesus heard the beat of certain wings in his brain. Where he heard the translucent, bone-white comfort of the dove, I saw the falcon of my malice.

This flex of John's madness met the aristocratic narcissism of the carpenter's son, as it will in any such collision, with profound agreement. The petty cruelties I had set upon Jesus' confidence in our childhood had convinced him, as he grew better than I, that I was jealous of him. I set him up to believe that I was a runt fox, envious of his lion's power, but, in truth, until John—sunblind, crippled by frustrated sexual desires, and insane from the white noise of the Jordan and the river at Bethany—gave his final flattery, Jesus had not known how to sustain this belief. He required others, vindication. I realized that he would now take it from whoever would offer it, and that the previous night where he had stepped onto the sandbar and fabricated a miracle meant, he would do anything to foster it. He also knew that I was his problem.

"I saw the sandbar," I whispered to him as we walked that evening. Letting Jesus have that first miracle set all else in chain. I could have told Simon and Andrew, he realized. He wondered why I did not. As it was, he would have to keep me close. Therefore, he made me treasurer of his disciples. I held the purse strings in his kingdom come.

"John told us that you are the Lamb and the Son of God," Simon enthused as they hurried along behind us, after we had left the Baptist and the spattered pulp that had been the priest Zeev. "Andrew says that we have found the Messiah."

"What do you want from me?" Jesus turned around and opened his arms, spreading out his palms at the level of his hips, as he would continue to do at such moments.

"Rabbi, we wish to stay with you. Where are you staying?"

"I will show you where we will stay." Already, he had Simon, whom he called Cephas or Peter—which means rock—and Andrew, and with money from their fish sold at market, Jesus rented a new house in Bethany.

The following morning, while Peter and Andrew were out in their skiff, I walked again with Jesus on the shore of Galilee. It was a beautiful morning, with white gulls floating on the sea. A man came shimmering out of the heat haze and started toward us, as if to speak. Jesus traced the shape of a fish in the sand with his toes. The man stared at it for a moment, and then he removed his sandals and extended his foot, drawing an eye in the simple outline of the fish. It was our code, agreed with Peter and Andrew, that meant *I am He*. And the opening of the eye meant *I recognize you*. Jesus looked at the man who had drawn the eye and said: "Follow me?" Wordlessly, the man fell in beside us as we walked. His name was Philip, and he was also of Bethsaida and known to the fishermen. The purse was heavy when we had sold the morning's catch and were roasting some of the remnants in our clay oven back at the new place where we were staying. The house was rich with new fish. We passed wine around, and our minds became full of inert erotica, passions that pulled like toothache, ambitions and myths of our endurance. Unconsciously, we pouted, fidgeted, and tested ourselves as the wine sank in, making fists inside the cuffs of our clothes, harkening to the kestrels in our blood, and seeing something in our futures other than abject horror as we soared above the earth.

Philip sat cross-legged close to the oven, pinching the yellowing blisters on his feet, letting the water out of them. He ran his hands through his black hair, sweeping it back from his face, which that was as round as a moon. He passed me the gourd and said: "Is it true that your father is a zealot, Judas? Has he killed many men?"

"Perhaps. But who of us really knows their father, or their mother?"

"Do you know the son of Talemai? Nathaniel?"

"The idiot savant. I see him almost every day beneath his fig trees, sweating and counting the fruit."

"He told me once that your father had killed nine Romans, and that boy can count." Philip smiled. "He can keep a secret too, when required, it would seem."

"What man are you talking about?" Jesus came over to us and sat down on the clean floor of the house. His eyelids were rosy from wine, but his gaze was still and unblinking, like a painted puppet of himself.

"Nathaniel. A young man who would follow you."

"Then we'll fetch him tomorrow. Will you bring him, Philip?"

"Yes, Rabbi."

When Philip found Nathaniel, he was beneath his fig trees, his lips moving softly in the dawn light. "Nathaniel, I have something to tell you. We have discovered him of whom Moses and the prophets wrote. He is Jesus of Nazareth, son of the carpenter, Joseph."

"Nothing good comes out of Nazareth, Philip. It's a cess pit."

"Why don't you come and see for yourself?"

I opened the door to Philip's knocking, and as the new man entered, Jesus took his hand and said: "Behold, Judas, here is an Israelite in whom there is no guile!"

"How is it that you know me?"

"I have seen you beneath your fig trees. I dreamed of needing men like you, Nathaniel." And Jesus spoke these things as though none of us had ever seen the young man before in our waking life.

"You are the Son of God, King of Israel."

Jesus said to him: "I told you that I saw you beneath your fig trees and so you believe in me? You will see greater than this. You will see the pastures beyond the brilliant blood-stained gates of Heaven where the cunning fail to enter. You will see angels cast men down and drag men up. And you will see a host of them descend upon the Son of Man." Between John the Baptist and this idiot, I reflected that things were going swimmingly, almost too good to be true.

He was without guile and stayed with us.

This was in the days when Jesus would still acknowledge Mary, his mother. Nevertheless, he was irritated and ashamed when she apprehended us on the street of whores. She looked like an emaciated bird in her blue dress and ivory scarf. The narrow bridge of her nose was red and flecked with scorched brown spots; it curled slightly toward her lips.

"J-Jesus! I have been trying to catch up with you for an hour now." She was breathless. "Did you forget your promise?"

"Woman, what in hell do you want?" he snarled.

"This afternoon is the wedding of Adiel and Chemda at Cana. You were invited weeks ago. Please do not embarrass me with your absence. Attend as you gave your word that you would, please."

"What is this wedding, and what are you or it to me?" His breath hissed through his clenched teeth as he gestured along the street of harlots.

"I am afraid of you, son." Mary looked at me then and asked: "Judas, is this cruelty, this dispassion, your influence?"

A wave of pity broke across my throat, and I strangled a strange and sudden sob that kicked there like a goat. The soles of my feet swung, for a moment, across a black and frozen abyss filled with all the despair of the universe. Poor woman to have such a son, I thought.

"The wedding, Jesus," I said. "We were invited, so we should attend." I regarded the tears streaming down his mother's face, the broken gleam of spittle on her lips. A million portraits and pieces of lurid trash graven with her image would never show her as she truly was: wracked with suffering, heartbroken, raving. In time, the truth of her womb would be removed by the terrifying hysterectomy of the New Testament, usurped by the dead uterus that Sylvia Plath called Vatican.

DOUBT AT CANA

We were late arriving at Cana. As the Gospel of John recalls, six urns of thirty gallons were consumed before Jesus and the disciples entered the scene. The trees were strung with garlands and lanterns, and the floor was spattered with vomit; the remnants of music were discordant, and the men and women had mutated into stained beasts. Adiel's family and guests numbered sixty, and Chemda's were forty; each had invited elderly grandparents, siblings, friends, and their children. That the large, resonant urns were dry meant that many of the wedding party had drunk two and a half gallons of wine each. The desire of these monsters for more poisonous vines came in terrible erotic convulsions; their teeth were black with it and their lendings abandoned to it, disheveled and torn. I thought of Hamlet describing his mother's love for his dead father: *She would hang on him, as if increase of appetite had grown by what it fed on.* So hung the wedding party from red tendrils of wine.

"There is no more," Mary, Jesus' mother, informed us.

"We have brought some," he said. "Fill the urns with water, and we will dilute our wine into it. Take some to the steward of the feast. He will not know the difference."

We discovered the steward dressed in the soiled uniform of the steward of the USS *Eldritch.* The brass cuff buttons had been chewed off by the girl he was with, who was now bent over a desk, splaying torn nautical maps and India ink, smashed instruments as their sex went on. The steward tried to pull up his white trousers but could not. The girl—Mary Magdalene in a platinum blonde wig, dressed as a cowgirl—shoved her flanks back against him, twisting her ornate boot heels into the dirt, as her sequined breasts swung and her Colt pistols and holsters floated about her hips. I handed the steward a flask more of wine, and he put it to his lips, saying, "This party just gets better and better." So it was with the others.

Later, as the disciples slumbered in pools of diluted wine, the rose hue of it absorbed into their clothes, I picked my path across the piles of entangled limbs, seeking Jesus but finding him nowhere. For a moment, as I exhausted the sockets of the building, I considered that he might have left us, soberly. I discovered him concealed alone inside the closet of the bridegroom. As I opened the door, light from the master bedroom clawed in over him. He was sitting in the dark, his arms folded around his knees, his head bowed beneath the curtains of hanging robes surrounding him. He looked up.

"Judas? The festivities are done? I—I was afraid they would find me out." I extended my hand, gripped his wrist, and pulled him to his feet.

"Find you out?" As he emerged squinting into the light, I smiled at him as though I did not understand his fear. I wanted to fill him with certainty. I brushed confetti from his shoulders, and Jesus scoffed also and shook his head.

* * *

WE STOLE donkeys from the paralyzed wedding and rode back to Capernaum, the Marys with us, and there we slept beneath the stars on the shore of Galilee where the moon was as grave as the omens in Oscar Wilde's *Salome*, a shining menstrual skirt with silver upon the water. When there was a wind, we sheltered beneath upturned boats: beetles in skulls. Mary cast her platinum blonde wig and green contact lenses across the water. I saw the Baptist's head on a platter and had many inspirations watching her gorgeous legs in the surf.

The Feast of Passover was close at hand, and Jesus spoke of spending it at Jerusalem, the *axis mundi*, the city of chaos, since Passover is the commemoration of the barbarism of the Lord. "I will not go with you for Passover," I told Jesus. "I am against it. It offends me that you can look in the eye of the God who will send an angel of death to pass over the homes of the Egyptians and kill all of their firstborn children. Slavery does not excuse such a vile massacre. Our land is now occupied by Rome, but I could have no God that would commit a spectral genocide against so many innocents in the name of my freedom. How dare you show gratitude for that? How dare you claim that privilege? You cannot turn a blind eye to it: we have no use for him."

Jesus went to Jerusalem. But in Jerusalem, his conscience was pricked. It was distasteful to take Scripture at its word, and if it were mere words, then there was even less reason to cling to it, committing sins of omission by not confronting the sickness within its decorous liturgy. The texts would be brought out, and the hallowed ghostly massacre of the Egyptian babies and children itself would be passed over like a haunted guilty secret. The children of Jerusalem would play Passover games of memory and counting plagues, but their parents would conceal the truth of the tenth plague from them. And so, he went to the Temple with great fury and confusion. My disgust was ringing in his ears.

"You trade on this?"

As Jesus passed into the Court of the Gentiles at the Temple, where mordant men sold pigeon meat and pungent spices, his voice was almost nothing more than a question unto himself. But by the time he had moved through the Court of the Women, where bright textiles flowed between jars of myrrh and trays of sweet baklava, into the Court of the Israelites, his voice was a scream. "You trade on this?" he cried until blood gathered in his larynx. Inside the hive of men there, some auctioned bloated oxen and sheep, others made loans and exchanged currencies, and others offered fried fish and street food. With a golden cord he had snatched from a stall in the Court of the Women, he fashioned a whip and thrashed at the oxen. The beasts ran riot, trampling bodies and smashing the market stalls. From the vortex of his fury, Jesus called out: "You will not make my father's house a place of commerce!"

"Bastard, your father was a carpenter!"

"This place will eat you alive!" Pharisees spat in his face as they fought to escape the stampede. "Blasphemy out of Nazareth, you will not be forgiven this. Two score years of building this Temple and you want to play blind Samson and pull it down on our heads! God and Herod will destroy you!"

Jesus punched his own chest. "Destroy *this* Temple and in three days I will raise it up again!"

Self-resurrection?

Jesus had gone too far beyond the bounds where I might indulge him. Yet, these regrettable theatrics informed me that he was, at last, absolutely convinced of himself and that his inferiority had gestated and swollen into this ultimate rejection of reality. His tormentor was but a shimmering smear at the periphery of his consciousness. He had almost forgotten that I dangled there, taunting, manipulating the strings of his puppet miracles. From the slights and insecurities of his childhood, I had constructed and coaxed a monster from those remains. Was he challenging me to murder him, to finish his abdicated self-killing? This Jesus labored beneath the misapprehension that he was the master of his own destiny and of mine. When disillusionment reached him, it would come brutally, mercilessly. I anticipated it with something close to joy.

JUDAS ISCARIOT, THE ASSASSINATION OF JFK, AND THE SUICIDES OF MONROE AND HEMINGWAY

November 22, 1988. The Vegas Club, a strip club in Dallas, Texas. Two writers, Norman Mailer and Barry Nathaniel Malzberg, are bivouacking there after fighting through the picket lines at the movie theatre to see *The Last Temptation of Christ* and Harvey Keitel's flame-haired Judas Iscariot. On this of all days, it seems appropriate. Previously, Malzberg has caused scandals with the almost simultaneous publication of his dystopian novels, the suicidal *Guernica Night,* where "the final trip" is offered to all reaching the age of twenty-one, and *The Destruction of the Temple*, revisiting the assassination of President John F. Kennedy. Later, Mailer will almost simultaneously publish his *Portrait of Picasso as a Young Man* and *Oswald's Tale.* Unconsciously, in the blacks of his unconscious, Mailer thinks of a novel that he will call *The Gospel According to the Son.*

Dead presidents, classical composers, and religious figures were the meat of science fiction writers, appearing as automata and simulacra in the novels of 1960s and 1970s radicals. Bourbon is flowing. Cigarette smoke fills the lounge as "All Along the Watchtower" plays on the jukebox.

"Here is to Abraham, father of all of us lost Brooklyn Jews."

"Yes, a toast to Abraham Zapruder."

"Abraham Zapruder, who came from the Soviet Union to Brooklyn, and then here to Dallas with his 8mm camera, to accidentally film the assassination of our greatest president, Jack Kennedy, on this day twenty-five years ago."

"And while Abraham Zapruder was settling in Dallas, after New York, Lee Harvey Oswald was unconsciously, inexorably, following him. I believe that in '42, Oswald was in foster care in New York before enlisting with the marines and defecting to the Soviet Union in 1959. Like the prodigal son, Oswald returned to Dallas in 1962 and found himself a job at the Book Depository."

"He was a marine who married a girl named Marina."

"He beat the shit out of her, too."

"Did you know that the Judas of Greenwich Village, Bob Dylan, his father was named Abraham, and he died of a heart attack on Jack Kennedy's birthday, five years after the assassination?"

"Kennedy was wearing a back brace that afternoon, so that when the first shot struck him and passed through his throat, he could not fall."

"This is the bar where Jacob Rubenstein met Candy Barr. Jack Ruby liked to carry a gun in a holster, a Colt .38, and Candy Barr's stripper shtick was a cowgirl gig, with holsters, boots, six-shooters, and platinum blonde hair like Marilyn."

"Monroe commits suicide three months after singing at Jack's birthday party; some say she had a secret abortion right after. Dead, she's apparently full of pills, but there was no running water in her room, and no glass. One year later Jack is killed, twenty-five years ago today."

"When Ruby shot Oswald, he was supposed to be jacked up on Preludin. Ruby thought he was injected with cancer cells in custody, and he died of a pulmonary embolism and was riddled with cancer."

"JFK, Lee Harvey Oswald, and Jack Ruby all laid out in Parkland Hospital."

"Behold the narrow gurney of the world!"

"I'll drink to that."

"Pernod!"

❖ ❖ ❖

1998. PROVINCETOWN to Armageddon. Before letting it fall, Norman Mailer pinched the shining nickel coin between his thumb and forefinger, leaning over into the black funnel where the full panoply of his ghosts spun roaring like motorcyclists upon the wall of death. He wondered: How close can one get without jeopardy to the soul, sucking the teat, hammering in the nails? Why should I write this? Where is the audacity in the known course? Is there a sting of vigor in sparring with the crude styles of Matthew, Mark, Luke, and the southpaw John, one piece of fiction taking on another for the provenance of the skull? Or is it all death? The novelist, like a pugilist winning on points as the rain thrashes his windowpanes in

Provincetown, raising the penitent belt over his head, asks if the writer is cheapened by repetition where the painter is not. I am not afraid; what is one more portrait of Christ? The coin kept falling and made no splash. The well was truly without end. He felt a quiet fizzing in his kidneys and a momentary souring of his breath. He thought of tall buildings in Brooklyn Heights, Washington, D.C., filthy machine gun mountains in the Philippines, the Texas School Book Depository, and the glass mountain of his reputation, of Lucifer haunting the high peaks, Lucifer the bright star of the artist and the egomaniac. Mailer thought of his Judas: Jack Henry Abbott stabbing a waiter in the heart in the East Village, secretly suspecting and willing that Abbott would one day hang himself inside a prison that moaned like a whale. The contracted belly of the universe, a song of infinite pain, stalled in Mailer's mind as he thought of how he might fail and write Jesus into heaven. Mailer poured a measure of orange juice from a cardboard carton into his glass of red wine. He was exhausted. After working at his words, writing about Judas, he fell asleep and dreamed of his idol, Ernest Hemingway. He felt himself switching skin.

Contemplating the moon-blue barrels of his shotgun, the old man recalled the fiestas of violence that his flesh had known. He saw bulls shift like black tornadoes, marlins opening the white waters of the capes, and virile shrapnel spread upon the hills of Europe like wasted youth. He had become an aficionado of death. He could hear the spooks closing in, the FBI rattling at his doors, the CIA tapping his telephone. The world was conducting a séance in his head. The metal of the gun tasted like old money.

THE GLITTERING SNAKE

Our wooden doors beat together in a storm, and rain wept through the lintel. Inside, by oil lamp, we—Jesus, Peter, Andrew, Philip, Nathaniel, and I, Judas—put our palms toward the small stove. Jesus told us of the violence at the Temple. Nathaniel, who remembered many things, recalled that it was written in the Psalms: "For the zeal of thine house hath devoured me, and the reproaches of them that reproached thee are fallen upon me," and we were much confused by the sense of the words. Lightning hung in the charged sky, and I regarded the single white hair that had appeared on Jesus' scalp.

"Do we have money for the market tomorrow, Judas?"

"Not much."

"If the storm continues, we will not be able to fish."

"Judas can pick pockets."

There came a knock upon our door. At first we took it to

be the wind, but then it came again, regular and fleshy from the fist in the street. And then we heard a man's voice, low in register, calling: "Rabbi, I am Nicodemus of the Sanhedrin; please permit me to enter."

I reached for my knife and whispered to Jesus: "The Judiciary, they have come after the outrage at the Temple."

"Rabbi, we *know* that you are sent by God. Signs and wonders—" Before Nicodemus could finish, Jesus strode across the room, tore open the door, and dragged him in, as though he were a shepherd yanking a sheep though a narrow gate. Nicodemus was a perfumed and beautiful man in middle age. "Master," he said, "master, no one can do these things, save you. God is with you."

"This is a glittering snake," I warned. "A flatterer from the Pharisees. They will draw you out."

"Nicodemus," Jesus spoke with infinite tenderness, as though he were soothing a child with fever. He placed both of his hands upon the Jew's shoulders, purple-black silk flowing between his fingers, myrrh emanating from Nicodemus' oiled and powdered skin; he reminded me of Herod with less money. "Favored Sanhedrin, known to all, I tell you that it is not enough to witness signals. Unless a man is born anew, he cannot see the kingdom."

"Be born? Return to my mother's womb? I cannot."

"You must be born twice, once into the red slime of the world, and then again, through clear water and the Holy Spirit. That which is born flesh remains flesh and cannot enter the kingdom of God. See the bloodstained gates. Only that which is delivered Spirit may enter as Spirit. I am midwife to history."

"I do not understand," Nicodemus complained.

"And you call yourself a teacher." Jesus spun on his heels and strode about the room. His chest heaved with contempt. Then he turned back and leveled his index finger at Nicodemus. "You comprehend not. Listen. *None* have ascended to heaven, save he who descended from heaven, the very Son of Man. And as your Moses lifted up the serpent in the wasteland, so must the Son of Man be lifted up, that whoever believes in him may have life eternal. He is not here as a weapon. He is here to save the world. But not to believe in him is death, the most abject death and a slaughter of the spirit, forever. The world is shrouded in the dark of men's evil. He has not time for stories. Believe . . . or die."

I watched a moth and her babies pour into our candle flame.

Now, John the Baptist was at Aenon, close to Salim, where the fronds of tall trees cast flickering light and shadow upon the tents and homes. Aenon was plentiful with water, where springs illuminated the yellow rocks and soft algae sent tendrils into the Jordan. John spent his nights in the cave Sapsaphas, where his shadow haunted him. His shadow was my brother Jesus, who also baptized close by. One night, Jesus and I visited John in his cave, lying down in the straw that he had spread there and eating bread and honey together.

"I am a friend to the bridegroom and rejoice to be overshadowed," John said. "More will come to you, and I will diminish, and this is as it must be. The Levite, Bud, informs me that the Pharisees already ask how you baptize, and they are concerned that you not become an influence. They intend to come here, warranted from Herod, and therefore you should leave, purchase more time."

"It is a pity, John," I told him.

Jesus left before dawn, traveling to Galilee, through Shechem, which is also known as Nablus, Samaria. Angled slabs tore out of the soil; trees splintered and blossoms sifted through the air; stone pillars projected from pools of fetid black water, and wolves howled in gardens of broken glass; and altars of gore buzzed in the morning sun. This had been the place where Abraham was given the land of Canaan, and the place where the children of Jacob avenged the rape of their sister, killing every inhabitant. On a small hill of grass, frame 313 of the Zapruder film was projected onto a fleece, stretched from ropes extending from the boughs of tall pistachio trees, and the trees were surrounded by disintegrating cigars, dollar bills, slimming pills, and strips of underwear. A woman was lying beside the well that was the well of Jacob. Jesus did not want to approach her, but his thirst was great.

"Woman," he called out, "draw me some water from the well."

The woman, who had been asleep, raised her face and squinted into the sunlight that was behind him. "Who are you to demand that of a Samaritan woman?"

"You should not ask, but you should give him water that asks, so that you may receive the living water of the Holy Spirit. Then, thirst will end. Go and fetch your husband and tell him this also."

"I have no husband," the woman told him, pulling her clothes about her.

"That is true. You can marry as many times as you have and still have no husband. All women are the brides of the Christ and not of men, or they are whores."

"How many husbands have I had?"

"Five."

"Huh. Is the Christ in Samaria, then?"

"I am he."

The disciples arrived at that same place then, and Peter was distressed to find his teacher conversing with the Samaritan woman. "Rabbi, John has been arrested, and we left Aenon in terrible haste, not even bringing food. Why do you tarry with a woman here? We must go!" I saw to it that the woman spread word of our passing there. The woman, who was as superstitious as my mother, told everyone she met that the Messiah had baptized her with the moisture of his breath, and that he had known deep into her heart. And, as Shechem was ruptured by a thousand woes, drought, massacres, and disaster, there were many who wanted to believe her.

When we returned to Cana, where the wedding had been, a man accosted us in the street. I knew him as the rope-maker Marcus. His face was streaked blue and bruised with tears. "Judas, Judas, which of these men is the one who turned the water into wine at the wedding of Adiel and Chemda?"

"It is he, the one who looks like a sleepwalker." I pointed to Jesus, who moved exhaustedly between the parrot stalls and the insect trays. "I will take you to him."

"Blessings upon you, Judas. My son, they say, will die of his fever within the hour! I cannot bear it."

"Jesus, this man is Marcus, the rope-maker. His son is sick. Dying."

Jesus flashed me a look that only I could see, because I was anticipating it. With his eyes he asked me: *dare I do this?*

"Marcus," I said softly, turning his body slightly away from

Jesus with the crook of my arm, "who is the doctor who told you that your son will die within the hour?"

"Asa, the son of Eliezer."

"Ah, yes, I know Asa," I told him. Then, I knew that this was a coin toss. Asa was a pessimistic young man, inexperienced with fever, and one wont to hedge his bets. I steered the rope-maker back toward Jesus and said: "My master will see to this," the words like bitter vomit in my throat, and I gave Jesus a delicate signal that told him that he had nothing to fear in projecting a miracle.

"Please come to my house before my son dies."

You dare do this.

"I do not need to. Your son will live, because you believe in me."

THE BATHS OF BETHZATHA

On Shabbat, we came to Jerusalem from the east, to the baths of Bethzatha with five porticoes. A blackening panther turned on a spit, sliced by the presiding Roman guards; a freckled man in a corset floated on his back, brain tissue protruded like a hernia from the right side of his skull, adrenal hemorrhaging killing his attempts to swim back to the tiled banks as he floated between the bloody heads of sheep that glared across the water; mutilations of failed suicides, leprosy, the half-murdered, a woman with a tumor bulging from her armpit with milk teeth and stiff black hairs; children with infected circumcision wounds swam ashamedly in the filthy currents; syphilitics smashed their brows against the stone pillars and collapsed unconscious into the shallows to heal or drown like witches; an algae of choleric vomit trailed below the surface, and excrement disintegrated in slow ripples behind the deformed, the diseased, and the dying. Several slumbered on collapsing piles of pallets, arranged with whatever towels and bedding that they could find.

I beheld him then at the midnight of his doubt.

"I cannot heal this!" Jesus gasped into my ear.

"You do not *want* to," I reassured him. "You are not here to heal the sick, for the *truly* sick you cannot touch."

Therefore, reflecting Skullhead, he went among them with his cyanide needles.

And certainly, there were many malingerers who, seeing the angel of death approaching, rose from their disgusting pallets and started away from him with cries of anguish. And he banished them from Bethzatha, calling: "Take thy bed and be gone!" And others he removed from their crippled misery by injecting them with cold, fatal potassium cyanide. This, I told him, was the crux of his aristocracy: one does not consort with whores and tax collectors for their own sake; one only does so because one believes that the shocking force of one's will, or violence, will stop them from being whores and tax collectors; this is not tolerance. As the malingerers fled from the screaming porticoes, they passed Jews who pleaded with them: "It is unlawful for you to carry your pallet on the Sabbath!" And the malingerers replied that they had been made to leave their place of sickness by a tall and terrible black-haired angel. The Jews resolved to discover this angel, but when they arrived in the bathing house, where the diseased lay dead upon the surface of the waters, Jesus had gone, and a wailing, red-eyed crowd was in his place. We fled into an alleyway where flies shot like pellets through the meat fumes, dust, and shadows. And in the same alleyway, we cornered one of the malingerers. Jesus stepped forward and the man forced himself into a crack between two houses.

"You see, you are not sick," he said, and his words trailed with soundless but furious screaming as the tail of the comet that hung over his birth. "Abandon sin, that nothing worse than I visit you."

"Master, I will, but who are you to clean out the cesspool?"

"I am the lamp at the summit of the earth, and where my light falls, all burn."

Later, in the early evening, we were accosted by one of the black insects of the Sanhedrin, saying: "I believe that I know you. Myself, I mean you no malice, but if you work on the Sabbath, you cannot but bring the wrath of the Jews."

"My father works still, and I am working."

"You do not mean Joseph the carpenter."

"No. And I tell you that I do nothing, *nothing,* by my own volition. I am a shuttle in the loom. Another hand moves me. For the hand loves the shuttle, and the shuttle knows nothing but the hand. For, as the Father raises the dead from the soil and gives them life, so the Son lets live whom he will. All judgment and disgust are in the Son who does his Father's work. Therefore, those that honor the Son honor the Father. I stand at the sheep gate and let few beyond. And the hour is close where the sheeted dead will gibber in the streets of Jerusalem, and across the earth, splitting forth like grass, and I will move amongst them with a scythe. The entombed will claw from their discrete canyons, and I will part the field of the good and the evil without mercy."

"You do not bear false witness?"

"Should I bear false witness and play the unfaithful bridegroom, my blade will be blunt and I shall be overwhelmed. Carrion birds will chew me off the altar. The one who sent John the Baptist sent me, as prophesied. John was one lamp that burned bright in the wasteland, and for a time, there was much rejoicing in his radius. There is a lighthouse at Alexandria. My gaze, that is a million suns, as an annihilating passion, makes this lighthouse a dull and fleeting spark from one poor anvil of man. You have not yet seen light. When a false prophet announces himself in the name of man, you are lenient and even tempted to follow him. Yet, when the Son announces himself in the name of the Father, you scurry from the lamplight to the shadows, seeking solace in the scriptures of man. Moses warned you about me, and now Moses condemns you in your disbelief! I will accuse you to the Father, for if you cannot believe the writing of Moses, then you cannot believe in my words. You pay lip service to Scripture and secretly hope that all is false while you live in the aristocracy of your false spirit! As you scorn me this moment, you will be scorned eternal."

"Rabbi, you are right, and I do not desire the end of the world. I have witnessed many men claim to be the Messiah, and each time, I rejoice in his delusion, for I know that we are truly saved, not by his coming, but by his absence. It cannot and must not be true. I do not believe that you are the Messiah, but I suffer that you are the closest and latest."

And Jesus said: "That is not enough."

And the Sanhedrin said: "It will suffice. I will grow into an old man, and keep a quiet counsel, long after you are crucified for sedition."

THE BIRTH OF JESUS

That night, as I slept in the bed beside him in the house that we rented, Jesus shivered in his dreams and the blood-straw circumstances of his birth, the death plunge of the comet, the hot breath of the oxen, the luxuries his father had stolen in order to build a new life for Mary and himself, Joseph, master carpenter and cheap cuckold. There he lay, born between beasts and the sparkling promise of the occult in the night sky. My mother had watched the comet also . . . *Sweet Judas,* she crooned, as I began to slip from her womb. The umbilicus was about my throat, the guilty cable of her body seeking its moment. Her cunt contracted on my neck. My feet kicked and my body twisted there, and I escaped the death that some perverse part of the world desired for me. And one escape demands another, and even the asphyxia of Houdini does not kill the spectacle, the revolt against the casts and caskets of our being.

We went to the house of Zebedee, an old man full of rage at his coming death, and his wife Salome, who was the sister of Jesus' mother Mary and midwife at his birth. We would have their twin sons James and John follow us.

"Please do not take my sons with you," Salome pleaded. "In a dream I saw the sword of another Herod cutting them down, and Jesus too. I saw your corpse in a wet cave, and I was anointing you with spices and oil because you had been crucified and lay in the poverty of death. Why would you destroy your mother?"

"I have none. I am come to end the work of women."

But Zebedee railed: "Take them! Make more than ash of them, and let one or both be martyred so that they will not fade and palsy like their father."

"I will give your sons the power to cast out demons," by which Jesus meant to forget their earthly parents and to see the world as ghostly and damned.

And the sons of thunder were desperate to leave their house.

We found Thomas, who had also been called Judas Thomas, the twin, working at his taxidermy business, where he fingered and stitched the wounds of the dead. A small bell sounded as we opened his splintered wooden door. A Levite gang had smashed their way in and stolen his scalpels and most of his savings, and now the floor was littered with mutilated owls, torn cats, and hanks of the fleece stuffing that he used to preserve the animals. He was called *T'oma*, or twin, after rumors concerning the ghastly effigy of himself that he constructed by night. The floor was slick with embalming fluids.

"I have no more faith in men," he said, "but I will go with

you, since there is nothing left for me here. Would that I had
constructed a mannequin of myself; then I would have made
it keep vigil from my window by a single lamp to threaten the
bastards in the streets while I am gone!"

Also, we found Jude Thaddeus. We discovered him in one
of the bleak and labyrinthine places of the city, beating a
Roman sentry to death with his club. Alcohol fumes shrouded
him. "Be careful that none of us are seen here," Jesus warned.
Jesus loved him, for Jude Thaddeus would follow a raindrop
to the floor of the sea and drown trying.

The rest of the twelve were Matthew the tax collector, whom
we kidnapped as he came rattling our door one night seeking
tithes for the Occupation; Simon the Zealot, who wore a knife
belt carved with the notches of the dead; and James, the son of
Alphaeus, who was simple and quiet as a shadow.

The Endless Feast

To my discomfort, word of the carpenter's son who could work miracles and who spoke with the obscurity and violent determination of a prophet spread rapidly as ink; the indelible and confused Rorschach of his reputation went out before him, so that when we went to the other side of the Sea of Galilee, which is the Sea of Tiberias, a vast and muttering crowd followed behind us, believing that they had seen and would see the lifting of disease, the straightening of twisted limbs, and the washing clear of cataracts with a breath. We looked back at the city, the jaundiced abutments and projections, the soft and crumbling sandstone, and the red dirt blown up from the marketplace. I walked at the head of our twelve, and many of those behind us assumed that I must be the Messiah and would call out and wave their arms at me in supplication. "Lord, thou art beautiful," they cried. "Stop and speak with us."

In silence, I climbed a great hill, listening to rubble cracking and falling down behind, and the multitude went after me, until I reached the summit with the twelve, and all others fell still before sitting down on the hard and gritted slope. Then we also were seated on the ground, except for Jesus, who stretched out his arms and in the rising sun sent a black shadow down into the valley. The people who had called out to me were ashamed and experienced the fear that came suddenly to the goats that had followed my traitor goat to the killing place, the bloody tree in Kerioth where I had come from.

"Judas here is our treasurer," Jesus addressed them, pointing to me. "How much money do we have, Judas?"

"None," I said, shaking my empty pouch.

"How much would it take to feed these who hunger?"

From below us on the slope, an aged voice called out: "That boy there, he has a spit of six dried fish on his shoulder. And I have one hunk of bread in my sleeve!" The boy stood up and danced in place, waving his spit of fish over his head. The people laughed together. And when the old man held up his fistful of stale bread, the people cheered him.

Another in the crowd cried: "You see: even if we had two hundred denarii we would all still go hungry. And besides, comfort does not go where it should."

"Sit down, sit down," Jesus urged, and as the old man crossed his feet again, he wondered how he had not noticed the luxurious grass beneath him before. "Man deceives himself with so much concern for nourishing his flesh. Let each of you take one flake of fish from this boy and one crumb of bread from this old man here and *know* that the soft and watery sounds from your bellies are as nothing to the crying and howling of your hungry ghosts in flames if you do not feed your spirit. Gather the fragments, and let nothing be wasted here! I am the bread of life, and he who believes in me shall know not hunger nor any thirst."

Simon the Zealot whispered: "Rabbi, there are spies here, a glint of metal in the crowd."

"A sword?"

"Perhaps."

A woman called out: "Some of us here know you as the son of Mary and Joseph. How do you now tell us that you are descended from heaven?"

"You who speak of mothers and fathers," he answered, "your mothers and fathers ate manna in the terrible wilderness and they perished in knots of empty agony. Here is the bread of heaven, sent that those who eat of it shall know life eternal. If anyone eats of this bread, they shall shirk death and live forever. The bread that I give for the life of the world is my flesh!" The morning sun sent a red smear across his face.

The Jews did not understand.

"Cannibalism?" They knew of the mythology of the god Pan, who also taught with wine and who was torn in pieces and devoured by his disciples, blood flowing through their teeth as they hunted him on the mountainside. "How can you give us skin and blood to eat?"

"Truly, truly, I tell you: unless you eat the flesh of the Son of Man and drink his blood, you have no life here or hereafter. But he who eats of my flesh and drinks of my blood will be raised up on the last day of the universe. Repeat this when you return to your synagogues at Capernaum."

"This man is a demon!"

Jesus climbed upon a rock to better cast his eyes over the multitude. "There are some of you who do not believe. You are so made that you never shall. You are not at fault, because the Father does not *allow* all men to believe."

"Why?" The boy who had brought the fish heard this and asked with great concern and sadness. "Why is this?"

"Some of you are going to die. Even cities will be damned where I am not heard."

And a wave of pain and disgust passed through them all, as wind passes through a field of grass. It was a morning of great disillusionment and confusion, and it was the morning when the twelve were scattered. In the chaos and incongruity of that grassy knoll, we had gone as far as we could without a script. All conspiracies flowed into one river of turbulent screaming. I swam within it. Attending closely to him, I sensed Jesus beginning to swoon. I reached for him, wrapping one arm about his waist and pushing my shoulder under his, so that he hung on me in half cruciform as he spoke. "This is an evil generation." He tried to call out, yet fear constricted his throat so that these words came as a whisper to my ears alone. Jesus stared out over the multitude. To him, they had become a jellied swarming of eyes and a gnashing of teeth. He saw the demonic lump of thousands of men, women, and children spreading beneath him over the lilied grass. It was a tumor congregation of scorpions, serpents, and fish with parched mouths. He was struggling for new words. I perceived the ache in him to cast a net of compassion and love over the mass, and his shame at the bile that rose within him with each new attempt. Jesus raged against the realization that love had its limits, even in he who desired to treat the world in a way that he had not been treated. And I knew that his fear and suspicion of me had grown into a fear and suspicion of all.

"I am *confused*, Judas," he said. He spoke the word with the disbelief that I had heard actors portray when they say I am *poisoned*, or I am *dying*, or I am *killed*. Upon the green hill, he was like a wounded man with no one to seek sympathy from, save for the one who wounded him. A silence engulfed us, sealing us in like a transparent eggshell while the world roiled outside. Jesus' face contorted with hatred against me. He gritted his teeth so fiercely that I thought I heard them cracking. And his tearing eyes asked: *How did I get here? Judas, you brought me to this!*

The Motorcade

The first of twin American catastrophes that would hold the world on a pin: Marilyn rode him like a hurricane of silk, the cranium exploding like a shower of silver coins, traces of red in her hair as she blew him a kiss from the scaffolded birthday. I have his brains in my hand. Bob Dylan whined on a distant transistor radio. Abraham! Autumn shades of his scalp, the fall and flow of blood-soaked ticker tape. Shell casing shucked from moon rocket and bullet. Lincoln's scalp flapping like the hood of some blue-black automobile that bore his name.

In Dallas, jackals careened about the passenger door. Scarlet broth ran down her sunglasses. His back brace held him corseted to his cross, and the shot pealed again. Sometimes I forget that I am flying and then look out the aircraft window. The motorcade was a rolling tombstone. Traveling slower than the bullet, the sound arrived late, after his throat had opened like a Bible. The audience contracted and began to split, a serpent skin of Mylar, nylon, denim, fabrics of the future. The sky is as blue as old meat. No matter how many times I fly into New York, the atrocities still catch me in the intake of sky. The sun has died many times; the night is cold—what technique. Do the dead know what time it is? How many dead or alive?

Time is overlain, superimposed; mariners are fused disgustingly with the bulkheads and cupolas as the ship materializes again. Planes fly into buildings; firemen swim like cripples in dry rubble; policemen weep in some lunar landscape; fully grown we send our groggy spawn into the wasteland, stumbling from the wreck in asbestos crowns—the difference being that the Kennedy assassination, the Zapruder film, is a historical event; the crucifixion of Christ is a literary event; the testament is an exquisite corpse, the edited and confused messianic body. Out of the ash I come with my red hair.

The myths must be domesticated.

THE BROTHEL IN BETHESDA

The autopsy of John F. Kennedy took place at Bethesda
Naval Hospital, Friday, November 22, 1963. He was
embalmed at Bethesda. When I think of Jesus, I remind
myself: "I have his brain in my hands." Sometimes, I think of
Oswald's biblical opacity:

> REPORTER: *"Did you shoot the President?"*
> OSWALD: *"I have not been accused of that."*

Jacob Rubenstein ran a brothel in Bethesda, frequented by
Pharisees and Levite gang members. His favored moll was
named Candy Barr. The brothel had a saloon area downstairs.
I, Judas, and my brother Jesus were seated at the bar close
to Rubenstein—behind it, tending—and his girl crooning at
him over an untouched martini.

"Ruby, this drink is so dry. Is there nothing sweet behind your bar?"

"Oh, she's a smartalek, see?" he said to us, nodding in her direction. "Here." He dropped a cherry into her glass. "And here are some Turkish sweets from the fucking Arabs. Sheesh! I swear they're smothering me."

Candy Barr looked through Jesus as though he were a transparency, her eyes doleful and despondent, a woman frustrated by a half-glimpsed ghost, not suspecting how fully she would one day realize him when incarceration and fear had beaten her down. The dirt floor was strewn with disintegrating rose petals. The bar was painted yellow to crudely suggest gold. Behind it, behind Rubenstein, was a mural of a black stallion. Rubenstein called Candy Barr "the foxiest piece of ass in the Levant," a platinum blonde possessed of a Babylonian voluptuousness.

Jacob Rubenstein was riddled with cancer, bright spores foregathered in his lungs, silent, unknown. His hair was thin yet neatly palmed back from his brow, which joined the arc of his nose, hooking down like some stylized bird or one of the harpies of William Blake. His mood swung like a hanged man from the comedic to the violently grotesque. The unconscious suspicion that his death was not to be a distant episode rendered him by turns fearful, paranoid, and gregarious.

"You know who has the shortest life expectancy in any Roman legion?" he asked. "It's the schmuck who carries the Eagle!" He laughed and threw his large head back, coughing.

"Last week," he began, subtly indicating a shadowy gang in the corner of the room as he wiped a glass, "I heard a rumor that some Levites were ambushed up in the hills, surrounded by bandits. The bandits told the Levites that they might be spared and allowed to go free if they surrendered the leader of the gang."

"What became of them?" Jesus asked.

"You know that the leader of the pack wears the fanciest leather jacket, right? Well, he knew, and most of the others conceded that he had worked too hard to get that beautiful leather jacket. So, the Levites secretly drew lots and swapped their jackets, so that one of the whelps was taken instead. They dressed him up like the main man, and the bandits were satisfied in killing him. They flogged and shot him with stones against a tree."

"They were satisfied," Jesus said.

"The feebleminded make totems of other men. Wars are waged against abstract kings, leaders, and the notional states of man. Yet, it is true that the death of a king can assuage all the pain, the unremitting fears and disgusts of entire nations. Or, like the Romans pursuing zealous guerrillas into the mountain caves, they want the figurehead, as if killing him would avenge the worst insults and end the carnage of all their superstitions. Kill the king, smash the designated figurine, and all the foul enigmas of war and violence and conspiracy might end. So go the dreams."

I held Jesus by his elbow and explained to him: "What men desire is a King of kings."

Jacob said: "One final schmuck to bear the Eagle into Eternity."

But Jesus' eyes were fixed upon the television images jerking to and fro from the dying set across the high corner of the bar. On the grimy screen, a motorcade flashed in and out of existence.

"What a thing it would be to arrive in Jerusalem like that!" he said.

"Yes, you on a donkey!" Ruby laughed again.

"What the world desires is a scapegoat," I said. "When one of the boys from Bethesda took out a centurion's eyeball with his slingshot, the tetrarch made certain that a boy, any boy, was arrested immediately and his eye put out in kind: atonement not by the culprit but by the innocent. It has a potent hold over the people. It calms the garrison's nerves to have taken an eye for their eye. You see, Jesus, at times, the more meaningless and misplaced the retribution, the sacrifice of whatever lamb is at hand, the better to still the blood of the offended and to cancel the guilt of the many. What the world demands is a universal scapegoat."

A voice called out from the television static above the bar, sounding like a man drowning in ants. "They're taking me in because I lived in the Soviet Union. I'm just a patsy!"

And so, at dawn, we entered Jerusalem in triumph. The Levite gang leader Nitzan, or Bud, rode a Triumph *Tiger*: the kind of wild horse that had thrown Bob Dylan and that had lain burning bright in the forests of Woodstock. The large cyclopean headlamp of his machine probed into the remaining shadows of the night, and the 500cc engine roared our arrival. Others in the gang rode motorcycles called *Trophy*, the same ridden by James Dean. The chrome machines of the Levites reared up like furious horses as they cranked their throttles open, hosts of studded leather jackets shining in the sanguine morning sun. Some would roar ahead and then bank sharply, rear wheels sending wings and waves of dust into the air before returning to the pack. I walked at the front. Jesus was back in the midst of it, riding a young donkey, swathed in a blanket of red, white, and blue. For the moment, he was invisible, obfuscated by the grit of the road, the smoke and mirrors of the motorcade. I remembered the imaginary city that I had teased Jesus with in our childhood. The titanic glowing blocks of the Western Wall were interspersed with scripts and weeds.

The ticker tape began to fall, at first a few flakes and coils and then a steady stream of paper fragments. It filled the streets, resembling the chaff-covered floor of the carpenter's studio in our memories. It blew in clouds behind the Levite motorcycles. I bent down and grasped a fistful of it, all shreds threshed off the bodies of liturgy, as soon Jesus' flesh would be strapped and scourged from his torso.

JUDAS ISCARIOT AND THE SUICIDES OF
SAUL AND HIS ARMOR BEARER

I stared out across the battlefield from borrowed eyes. One thousand years before, since I had traversed into anachronism through hanging, I was Saul, first and cardinal king of the Israelites, a leader of donkeys but anointed to become leader of men by Samuel, the rebel judge.

"Saul, King." It was the voice of my armor bearer, high and thin on the wind beside me, barely more than a child. "Please, my Lord, let our eyes be sharp."

Mount Gilboa was awash with blood, scrawled with entrails, and blocked with corpses. Within the gore and trampled irises of the slopes, three of my elder sons, Abinadab, Jonathan, and Malchishua, lay dead. Though I was still abstracted from them, I was aware of the grip of grief in my chest. Philistine arrows stuck from their graying bodies. I could hear my armor bearer pleading with me again as my eyes flickered between the falling ticker tape as Jesus and I entered Jerusalem, and the cascade of deadly splints raining from the Philistine archers massed about us on Mount Gilboa. Suddenly, they set in place, and with that a terrible awareness of my existence as Saul, leader of the Israelites, flooded me with pain and confusion.

"Lord," the youth entreated me again, "though the Philistines have defeated you, remain, and be as our king, with strength and dignity in warring. Take heart."

"Boy, do you not see that despair has entered my pores?"

"Saul, King, I see only the bloodstained face of my Lord, once a herder of the tribe of Benjamin, and I remember well the ruthlessness of my king who massacred the Ammonites, who wiped out the Amalekites!"

"Yes, I remember the work. The placenta was still wet on the babies as we slew them and their mothers and as we killed the men, the runt animals, and the aged."

"You were king, in spite of God! And you stood with and also firm against the agent David, whom God sent from the treacherous tribe of Judah."

"True, I lent him my armor to face the monster from Gath, Goliath. We loved and hated David, held him close, and hunted him in exile. He brought me two hundred Philistine foreskins to buy marriage to my daughter."

"And he sought to murder you! He failed, and here, you live, despite God. Live now, and live again."

"I cannot."

"My Lord." The boy began to weep.

The Philistines massed about us, teeth frothed with spittle, short swords dripping upon the scarlet grass.

I took the boy's shoulder. "Last night, I consulted the Witch of Endor, in the black trees of the summit. She summoned the shade of the judge-prophet Samuel. And the hag and the ghost told me that I would die here today." I thought of the engraving of my collaboration with the witch by Gustave Doré. I thought of Custer, the red-haired Son of the Morning Star, surrounded by the Cheyenne and Lakota, putting his revolver to his heart. "Now, take my sword and run me through the chest," I commanded the boy, knowing that he could not do it. The boy shook his head silently. An arrow tugged through my sword arm, and the boy cried out. I passed my sword into my left hand, pressing the hilt against a stone, and I pushed and pulled myself onto it. Impaled on sorrow, like Ajax, I watched the boy do the same. And then I saw the witch, hanging in the darkness.

Bud, leader of the Levite motorcycle gang, called back over his black leather shoulder: "Rabbi, you can't say that Jerusalem doesn't love you." From all vantages there was celebration, and the Roman soldiers let us enter unmolested, despite the orgy of joy inspired by our engines. All the while, in the center of the motorcade, Jesus rode solemnly on his donkey.

As the motorcade went on into Jerusalem, I thought also of the suicidal King Abimelech at the siege of Thebes. I saw him running at the burning Theban gates at the brink of taking the city, when at last a woman forces a millstone over the ramparts, which smashes the king's skull like clay beneath a hammer. His armor bearer hastens to his side, staring stricken at the hanks of bloody hair and the hemisphere of bone hanging at his master's face. "Boy, you must help me take my own life. Help me with this sword; I am too weak, but let me not die by a woman's hand . . ." I thought also of Ahithophel, astrologer at the court of King David and grandfather of Bathsheba, hanging himself in despair; and of Zimri, who betrayed and murdered his master King Elah to become king of Israel for seven days before immolating his own palace and burning himself to death inside it. Market traders came forward and gave us food and wine.

"This will be a good supper, eh, Judas?" Nathaniel said.

We stayed several days in Jerusalem before the end came.

There were several suppers, where I told the others who remained of the twelve of acts of their master that only I had witnessed, since I was his brother.

THE OCCUPATION OF GERASENES

One time, we went to Gerasenes in the east, where Jesus had learned of a man possessed by a profound darkness. At the edge of the city was a great necropolis, with innumerable tombs and graves slanting in the vivid sunlight. The city itself, a place of pale amphitheatres and columns erected under the Roman Occupation, was haunted by the possessed man who, by night, howled in the graveyard, clawing up clots of earth and snapping the bones he found beneath with grotesque muscles and terrible strength. Sometimes, it was rumored, he would run as fast as men imagined that an angel may move, his blackened loins beating against his foul powerful thighs and abdomen. His arms appeared to be filled with ships' ropes, and his eyes wheeled a hurricane of grief, a vortex of dying stars. He was a necrophile and a cannibal. All hope of imprisoning him had been abandoned. He had ripped garrison soldiers' arms from their sockets, and he spread his excrement on the pale tombs in the moonlight. He broke any chain that could be put upon him. The citizens of Gerasenes entreated us not to visit the sepulchers after sundown.

As we passed between the white stone columns that marked the gate, we smelled the human soil that had been spattered upon them. The moon lit a cloudless sky, so that despite the late hour, it was as dusk to us. Jesus abandoned his lantern, as I did mine. He moved with deliberate heavy footsteps, scuffing the dirt, intent on arousing the possessed man from his reeking cave. And soon, he was upon us. He was as tall as Samson and black with the decay he cavorted in. I felt for my dagger. But Jesus lunged forward and gripped the man by his hair.

"Are you possessed of an evil spirit?" Jesus demanded.

The giant roared, rolled his head, and stepped back, leaving Jesus clutching the revolting hair that had pulled from his scalp. Without another sound, the creature fell at Jesus' knees.

"Demon inside this man, tell me your name!"

"My name is Legion, because we are so many." He was possessed a thousand times, and he was a metaphor for Rome. The bats clung inside the belfry of his head and chewed the fat on the rungs of his ribs and did not want to be expelled from their occupation.

"Demons! I send you out of this man in the name of God, my father!"

At this, the demons exploded from the man's mouth and sought new refuge, entering a large herd of pigs that was close at hand. Jesus then pursued them until the animals fell from the crags to a lake far below, where they were drowned in the moonlight.

I taught Jesus to look below the surface, to look behind mirrors, to be witness to his own exquisite passion, without exposing it as mine. In this way, he might be the revolutionary to destroy the Roman Occupation, to drive the legions out. But the people of the city were afraid and angry that their pigs had been driven to their death, all to leave one hapless man shivering in the graveyard.

THE ASSASSINS AT BABYLON

Meanwhile, Jude Thaddeus had become dispirited and confused. He left us and went east to Babylon, the city between the rivers Tigris and Euphrates that is also called Babel. He sojourned in the hanging gardens of the feral King Nebuchadnezzar II, who had once driven the Jews from Jerusalem, five hundred years before. This was also the place of the abandoned great ziggurat of Etemenanki that some know as the Tower of Babel. Simon the Zealot also came there, since both men sought confrontation and were not patient with the narrative trajectory of Jesus. Jude Thaddeus went with his nail-studded club and Simon the Zealot with his skinny knife and belt of kill notches. They climbed high inside the ziggurat and camped there, watching the lamplights of the city, the Persian lanterns in the arched and vaulted gardens, and the candlelight in the mud homes. They lit no fire but remained warm inside black fleeces and shawls, hidden in the

night, plotting from the decaying balustrades and promon-
tories of the tower. They spoke in whispers, careful that their
words were not amplified by the resounding stones.

"This was the city of Nebuchadnezzar, who waged war on our
tribes," said Jude Thaddeus. "The same king who set up gold
as his god, and whose fornications rotted his sex and sent him
mad into the caves and dung of his old age, dog-nailed and
ruined. He became part wolf, like the vile suckling twins of
Rome. This tower, unfinished, is testament to the righteousness and power of our Lord against all of those who would
oppose us."

"Yet, Jesus hesitates. He meanders and shrugs close to the
wall like a virgin ignored at a wedding." Simon grazed his
knife along the granite balcony, keening the edge. "I think
that we were chosen because he wanted us, with a stomach for
the fight, to run where he feared to walk. To dirty our hands,
in contrast to his continual anointments."

"He sends his followers back to the synagogue, when he
should be sending them to war. For better or worse, the fist
changes more than philosophy." And holding out his club,
Thaddeus said: "There is no better argument than this."

"Tomorrow, we will seek and destroy the two Abyssinian
sorcerers Aphraxat and Zaroes. Now we are assassins for the
word," Simon determined.

The following morning, Thaddeus and Simon came down
from the tower and went quietly to the hanging gardens that
were a wonder of Babylon. They moved softly through the figs
and fly traps, the tuberose and orchids. The vines pulsed ichors

about them. There, in the gardens, Aphraxat and Zaroes kept a pair of tigers in a gilded cage. The sorcerers extracted milk and bile from the tigers with long, delicate needles that they would extend between the bars. When Thaddeus and Simon came upon the tigers, they were sleeping in the dawn sun. Their bodies heaved slow fire. Their breath was strong. The floor of the cage was stained with dried blood. With his thin dirk of a knife, Simon tampered with the locks on the cage, weakening them before he climbed into the canopy of creepers and flora, where Judas Thaddeus had already made cover.

When the Abyssinians came to the clearing where their tiger cage was, Simon whispered that they were as black as coals. The men had gashed rivulets in their cheeks and ivory hanging from their earlobes, and they wore cloaks of bright orange and black. Aphraxat approached the sleeping tigers, trailing his long fingers against the hardwood bars that held them from him. The animals raised their heads and flexed their feet, rising slowly. They walked with a bright and awful power, as of a forest fire. The Abyssinian pulled a key on a thong from within his cloak. Zaroes carried a sack of goat meat, buzzed with flies. The fly traps mouthed at them from across the arcade. It was the custom of the Abyssinians, each morning, to open the cage and to step inside to feed the tigers. Aphraxat opened the locks, barely noticing the way that the key felt looser inside the mechanism. The sorcerers stepped inside, and the tigers ate the meat from the men's hands, licking at their fingers. As usual, they stepped back outside the cage as soon as possible, before the appetite of the animals could increase. Aphraxat put his key back into the first lock. The key turned, but the mechanism did not. The dark men exchanged a look of confusion and disbelief. Again, the key turned uselessly in the lock, and the men began to speak rapidly. The tigers moved closer to the bars and the broken locks. Zaroes grabbed at the key to try it in another lock, and in doing so, he pulled the gate open and screamed. The pair of tigers roared from their prison, falling upon the two men and tearing them to pieces. Then they went about the gardens and streets of Babylon killing anyone that crossed their path. Simon and Jude Thaddeus ran behind them, crying out in joy and finishing off the wounded men, women, and children by club and dagger.

The pair of tigers fled the city, bloodied and sated. Some, in their terror, confused them with the disciples, who yet remained, shrouded in a miasma of gore and mystery. They came to the palace of the Duke Baradach. They panted at the palace walls.

"It was more than I imagined."

"It was a bloodbath."

Both men began to weep, exhausted.

They let themselves be seized by the palace guard and brought before the duke. The palace was filled with black idols. Baradach was engrossed in study of a large battle map that was spread out across most of the floor. Figurines of elephants and legions of soldiers were arranged upon it. His face was contracted with frustration. Without taking his eyes from the map that ranged into India, he extended his arm and pointed his finger at his captives.

"You set tigers upon my city and rendered my idols mute when I need to hear them most! Nothing speaks to me, not the ebony statues that house the gods, nor the priests, nor my generals, nor the beetles on the floor. You have set my city in shock. I am about to go to war, and you have put a silent plague upon us."

"Your idols never spoke to you," said Simon the Zealot. "You heard voices, but they were your own fancy. There are no voices but Jesus, the Nazarene."

"Liar! Let me set my cuff about your filthy mouth." Baradach walked across the map and struck each of them with the back of his hand. "What do you want?"

Jude spoke: "We could have gone on killing. We might have slain every beating heart in Babylon. But we come to you to die, murdering ourselves. You and your priests will live, and you will crucify us, knowing and fearing what we might have done, had we not chosen our death over yours. A holy war cannot be won. Therefore, martyrdom." And so the two were crucified, hanging from trees in Babylon.

THE ETEMENANKI HOTEL

Something had gone before us, a kind of notoriety, so that we passed easily through the checkpoint into the DMZ. Jesus and I enjoyed the streets. Journalists reclined in deck chairs or pivoted on cane seats, arranging themselves between the palm trees, where electric lights had been strung, and the graffiti metal barricades. They dressed in creamy linen suits, Panama hats, and sunglasses. They sipped coffee and cocktails, wiped sweat from their rosy necks, and looked nervously toward the slightest friction, as though waiting for the first detonation of the hydrogen bomb. A naked Persian boy moved between the geometries of deck chairs and outstretched espadrilles, shaking a mortar-shell casing filled with ice. "Martini, Martini, Singapore Sling strong enough to take down Goliath!"

A tank round had struck the Etemenanki Hotel during the night, and the literate internationals had been forced to lounge elsewhere. Part of the ziggurat structure of the hotel gaped and let in the indifferent morning sunlight, torn red drapes flapping from the fissure like strange tongues. Several ladies and gentlemen of the press, aid organizations, and political monitors had been killed in the blast, and now it was a somber morning of sunburn and stoicism. There were no miracles in the DMZ, no repeal of leper skin, no multiplication of food or unraveling of twisted limbs, only the louche certainty that the universe was without pity and that wine was less expensive than water.

And so, Jesus stood up before the journalists.

"The utterances of dark rooms shall be heard in the light," he said. "Privation's whispers shall be yelled from rooftops, the hypocrisy of Pharisees exposed. Of this world, report you well and truly. Comrades, do not fear the murderers of flesh, for when flesh is gone, what more can they do? Instead, fear the caretaker and harvester of all flesh who after he has killed has yet the power to cast it into Hell. He counts your eyelashes, the fronds of hair against your brow, weighs you, and wants to find you valuable. Yet, he will not always find you so. The angels of God will bar and prevent you if you do not follow me. Though you may libel me, this flesh Son of Man, you will be forgiven. But, blaspheme against the Holy Ghost and you will be tortured and torn asunder in eternity, as was Prometheus." A flock of black birds hung over the wreckage of the Etemenanki Hotel. "Consider ravens that neither reap nor sow. Yet, God feeds them."

"Are we to be as those carrion birds?" asked a young woman stenographer, adjusting her pencil skirt in the desert heat.

"And gamble the integrity of our bodies and brains on your afterlife?" spoke another.

"Nihilist," muttered an embedded military journalist.

I lit a cigarette and sat down in a vacant deck chair as Jesus continued to improvise for the multitude.

"Faithless ones. Do not ask whence your next meal, next drink, or your clothing will come, nor be wracked with anxieties over your survival in this world. These concerns are so universal as to be trivial. Surely, you have witnessed the hungry banality of all the nations of the earth? Instead, seek the Kingdom of the Lord. Sell your possessions and renounce kith and kin. Be a purse of flesh filled with an immutable currency that no thief may steal, nor no moth devour. For the end will come when you least expect it."

"Look at the hotel, Nazarene. Go and insult the dead there."

Then, as Luke tells it, Jesus in fury said: "I came to cast fire on the earth, and I wish that it were already burning! Do you *think* that I have come to bring peace on earth? No, I tell you! I have come to bring division! Father will be divided against son and son against father; mother against daughter and daughter against mother; all men against all women and all women against all men; skin versus skin! I will bring down tall buildings of flame upon your heads as I did at Siloam. I will permit no DMZ on this planet! Let the war be brought into every home and heart!"

With that, Jesus abandoned the journalists and swept on, deeper into the city of Jerusalem. He went hurried and sweating, and moreover, as the Gospels recall, he turned back over his shoulder and called out: "If anyone comes to me and does not *hate* his own father and mother and wife and children and brothers and sisters, yes, if he does not hate his very own life, then he cannot be my disciple!" Some who were walking after us halted in their tracks. "The law and the prophets were until John. Since then, the good news of the Kingdom of God is preached, and every one enters it violently."

"Rabbi," a young man called out, "if I hate my wife, should I divorce her?"

"Any man who divorces his wife and marries again is an adulterer. And any man who marries a divorced woman also commits the sin of adultery."

The young man also fell away in confusion and disappointment.

Some Pharisees who did not love bloodshed approached from the wings of the market, scattering monkeys and peacocks and spilling fresh figs from baskets. "Sir, you must get out of Jerusalem at once. Herod wants to kill you."

"Herod wants to kill me? That fox!"

"Forgive me," one of them said, in a tone of sympathy, "but I have witnessed prophets with scattershot revolutionary manifestos before, and you need not die here for such whimsical, violent talk."

"I will remain here in spite of Herod, the coward. For it cannot be that a prophet die away from his own land, even if it hears him not. O, Jerusalem, Jerusalem, murderer of prophets, stoning the messengers dispatched to your vaulted ears and womb. I would gather your forsaken children beneath my great wings like a mother hen gathering her brood about her."

Simon Peter and Andrew, who had been fishermen and were strong, caught up with us and pulled Jesus into a narrow side street, away from the crowds. "Master, please be careful."

"The days are coming when you will desire to see me," Jesus said, "but you will not. It is necessary that I suffer many torments and be rejected by this generation, right, Judas? Then, suddenly, I will bring apocalypse. It will be as it was in the time of Noah, when the world turned softly, and people lived their lives, ate, drank, married, bore children, and were content, until Noah closed the cargo doors on the ark and the Flood killed every one of the soft, drifting people. Noah did not look back. In the days of Lot, when the city of Sodom was destroyed with unspeakable righteous fire and rains of brimstone, so it will be when I unveil my apocalypse. It will be sudden. Remember Lot's wife. Do not look back. Do not try to save anything. He who seeks to gain his life will forfeit it. Of two identical men in the same bed, only one will be taken. Of twin sisters, one will remain. There will be such a night there."

"Where, Lord?" asked Andrew.

"Where the body is, there the vultures will gather."

In truth, the remaining disciples did not understand, but each feared to appear ignorant, and since Jesus had already told them that one of them would betray him, all feared the appearance of dissent.

The Empty House

We went about the city after nightfall, seeking an empty house to squat in, and we went to the district of the whores, where the chained hounds Gog and Magog kept guard at either end of the street. Where there were no lamps burning, I listened at the latches and windows, squinted through keyholes. Several times I found the lightless house to be occupied with sleeping whores, sometimes twenty sprawled upon pallets, glistening in the moonlight, a silver mist of sex rising from their bodies.

Finally, we found an empty building. I used my knife to pick the lock, and we hastened inside. Matthew, who had been a tax collector, put red veils in the windows, and James and John, the sons of Zebedee, poured oils into the empty lamp vessels. Thomas, who was also called Judas the Twin, found stale bread in a cupboard. Peter and Andrew worked with the cold coals of the fireplace. Nathaniel found some wine in a filthy bottle that he cleaned with his spittle and a portion of his clothing before pulling out the cork. Jesus reclined upon a pallet, watching. "We will need more food than this. Judas, you are treasurer. Will you go out and buy whatever you can? Tomorrow night will be our last supper together." I closed the door behind me and listened to the sounds of a chair being dragged against it as I inhaled the patchouli, wines, oils, and sweat of the night.

"Judas!" A voice came from the darkness in a stage whisper.

"Mary." Suddenly, I knew what I might buy.

I would proffer Magdalene all the money that we had in that tight purse, and in the morning, returning to Jesus and the remaining disciples almost empty-handed, I would recount how I had been robbed by drunken Levites and all the money had been stolen. Jesus would have no use for denarii, shekels, or silver soon, and I could always get more. Besides, did not his madness demand the surrender of wealth, property, materials, and the dissolution of earthly evidence? His words were that men should pass though the narrowest of doors, the eyes of needles and slits of fire, to deserve him. Magdalene took me to her new house where a redbud tree grew in a small courtyard, bloody blossoms spilling about and blowing against the low walls. She began to work with a series of locks that rattled in the moonlight. When I closed the door behind me, I heard eagles pouring through the smoking night toward roosts in the far hills.

Mary Magdalene's home was like a Gustave Moreau painting; I thought of his retellings of Salome dancing before Herod and the apparition of the decapitated head of John the Baptist, our friend, floating like a gory silver coin. It was a shrine to her sex, glistening with pearlescent light, tiger skin rugs from Babylon, black panthers, phallic ivory totems from Abyssinia, silver platters from Herod's landfill, Nazi lampshades of skin, Vatican censers hanging from golden chains fuming ghosts across the upholstery of the cherry divan. The room was perfumed with French neroli and hashish. An apron string hung from one of the iron bars of her skylight; I recognized it as the garter of the Queen of Sheba, swinging like a skinny serpent in the night breeze, a blue stripe across the bloodstained moon. There was a moth-eaten edition of Michael Moorcock's *Behold the Man* lying in a pile of pornographic magazines, Beardsley illustrations, and piss-smelling tarot cards. A platinum blonde wig hung beside a pink and blue Chanel suit. I ran my fingers through the dust on one of the cabinets. There was a carved wooden dove that Jesus had given her during our childhood. Beside it, a carved wooden whale named Leviathan and a painted wooden fly that she called Beelzebub. The whore stirred the embers of her fireplace, which flared and illuminated the blue and white Delft tiles surrounding it, Saul falling upon his sword. I sat down on the cherry divan, close to a stuffed black panther.

"That is some of Thomas' work," she told me.

"Judas Thomas, the twin and taxidermist. He will be useful in preserving Jesus' body."

She sat beside me, the red upholstery curling around her thighs like gelatin. Her hair was black and streaked with red henna, her skin pale but luminescent as a dying star, her eyes brown old coins. In her lap, she played with a length of milky

182 | JAMES REICH

cord, making knots and coils. Across the room, a phonograph
played, scratched and clicking like a Geiger counter.

At another time, my name was Bob Dylan. I was—and am,
and will be—a time machine of stolen skin, an arachnid,
and the skinny black face in your wallpaper pattern. I was
the secret sneer of God with a sheaf of psalms that you heard
about. You have collected evidence of me. You remember me
well as the wisp of gas across the president's desk, the glug of
the coffee percolator at the *Village Voice*, the jizz in Ginsberg's
beard, and every suicide note ever written. My story began
centuries ago, just a few years before I saw my best friend,
my brother, spidered on the cross. But in 1966, I was your
brothel-brained Jew-boy, spitting out anachronisms and Bible
characters, and the sleet of Manchester, England, stuck in my
hair like diamonds. My skull was a slot machine in Babel.
That night, I was still putting people on, flirting with disaster. I was a singer of songs, and I had been planning to sing
a new song, about my lost brother, Jesus. I had it tattooed
on my lips, and the vine of it stained my tongue. The lights
roamed around the auditorium, and I felt that I was in prison.
But, before I could sing it, someone fingered me with a name,
and they cried out: "Judas!" So, it is necessary to return to the
beginning. I heard myself saying: "Play it fucking loud!" like
a rolling stone.

"Turn that off. I can't listen to it anymore," I said to Mary
Magdalene. She stood up from the divan and went to change
the record.

"How about this?"

Love will tear us apart, again . . .

Mary returned and knelt in front of me, stellar and foxy, working at her knots. "Did you hear about Lazarus?" she asked.

Lazarus had become an albatross about the neck of the peasant town of Bethany, east of Jerusalem, where fig and olive trees were wrought in twists from the sloping soil. His little deaths, half-deaths, zombie dances, and somnambulist seizures brought fascination, terror, and a morbid tourism. "When my father was very ill," one of the Sanhedrin reflected, "in the poisoned places of my heart, I wished that he would die, and that the burden of his sickness be lifted from me. All Bethany must feel the same way toward Lazarus. He is an animated corpse, a taxidermist's toy, one piece of decaying meat." Mary Magdalene explained the anger toward Jesus, who it was said had intervened in the crisis and exacerbated the undead problem.

Lazarus staggered into the marketplace in his soiled bed-clothes, his red hair terrible as a cockatrice, his breath of tombs fogging in the early morning chill. The fishmongers waved filleting knives at him and told him to leave. Women covered their baskets of figs for fear of contamination. He appeared more ancient than ever. One of his teeth dangled from his lower lip, and a stained bandage was wrapped about his skull, holding one of his ears to his head. A stone struck him full in the face, knocking him down. Then, more stones fell upon him as the men and women of the marketplace cast their repulsion and rage at him. He lay in the dirt, a cloud forming about him as the stones thumped against his body.

His sisters, Mary and Martha, who had been searching for him since they found his sickbed empty, came screaming upon the stoning.

"Leave him alone!"

"We know you want him dead to make yourselves feel better! Bastards!"

"Cowards!"

The two women ran into the rain of stones and pulled their brother away, dragging his smashed form into a narrow street, before picking him up and carrying him between their shoulders, his feet pawing dumbly at the ground as though trying to walk. Lazarus groaned and cried, unrelenting tears pouring from his eyes, such was his pain and grief for himself and the world. He was death within his own body; he was his own iron maiden. Finally, Mary and Martha took Lazarus to the West Bank, his skin cracking like an old Van Gogh painting, fish-scale layers of bruises. From there two Egyptian fishermen who associated him with the myth of Osiris bore the broken body of Lazarus like crockery in their skiff to the island of Cyprus, where he died again. And across the Mediterranean, on Easter Eve, they smash crockery to stone Judas also.

I was still with Mary Magdalene, the night before the last supper. She put the milk-white noose that she had been making around my neck and threw the length of cord over a metal pipe that led to her cistern. The noose was soft and silken. She licked her bright red lips. With one hand she pulled lightly on the cord, tightening it about my throat, and with her other hand she expertly loosened my clothes on the cherry divan.

"Judas, how did you make Jesus follow you like this, to this suicidal Jerusalem?" Magdalene asked.

"Jesus is the passenger to my passion. I am the whip that moves the animal he rides on."

"What of the things he says?"

"He wants to hurt his parents. He is confused about his desires. Everything he has known—scraps of old prophecy, mockery, failures, beatings, the vagaries of his birth, rumors of his brother, the spell of John the Baptist that I exposed him to, the luxuriant deaths of his childhood idols—*everything* has given him a false sense that a life so abject must be secretly anointed."

"But what about you, Judas?"

"One only truly describes one's own heart by attributing it to another, and the greater part of genius is composed of memories." I was quoting Chateaubriand, writer, explorer, and lover of flesh, who had at first experienced Judea with revulsion.

As I said this, Magdalene's lips closed over me, and the fingers of one hand groped for the octopus of swollen tissue, desire, and agony that rolled and swelled behind my balls and at the bright nub of pleasure pulsing at my perineum. Translucent inks began to jerk through my loins as she rolled her tongue about me, and she increased the gentle pressure that she applied to the white noose about my throat. The noose sent me outside myself.

"In this world," she murmured, "sex and death are for time travel. Notoriety is time travel, permanence, to be at all times and all places simultaneously." She pulled harder and faster upon me, and the cord became tighter, closing my windpipe. I leaned forward to kiss her, cupping her breasts and wanting to wrap my legs around her head and to drag her back down to suck at me again. Desperation poured through my flesh. I desired only to explode in her mouth and hang in the blackout.

And I thought: they say that hanging is the death for women, witches, the treacherous, or for those men who forfeit their masculinity by base betrayals or murders in a cold rain of cowardice. The dangling man traverses the sexes. Suicide obliterates all gender and casts each corpse equal. The suicide is the necrophile's honey, each cadaver filled with sweetness, and hope spilling out, mysterious, erotic, unrequited . . . the pain in my throat disappeared. My head swam with sparks and dying stars, and come splashed white heat across Mary Magdalene's hands, wrists, and breasts . . . It smeared on my cheek as she loosed the cord and held herself to me. I knew that I was trying to die.

JUDAS ISCARIOT AND THE
DANGLING WOMEN

May 9, Mother's Day, 1976. "It is time to join the ranks of dangling women. From Macedon to Salem, few of us achieve it by our own hands anymore. Instead, it is the penalty passed down in the guerrilla war against God, whose name is Capitalism, and who killed more innocent children at Passover than the RAF at Dresden; and who is the destroyer of women. We have lost the war against money and shame. I ran away from my children, so I was called a witch. Later, I tried to kidnap my children and to smuggle them to Palestine for special education, but they were apprehended in Sicily. And I was called a terrorist."

Ulrike Meinhof committed suicide by hanging in her prison cell at Stammheim, Stuttgart. She fashioned a noose from the shreds of a towel and threaded it through the window grate. She hesitated a moment before kicking the stool from beneath her feet. She was an anti-Semite who justified herself by holding the fiction of Judas, the Treasurer, in her mind as if I were real.

Then, I was called Erigone, daughter of the Athenian shepherd Icarius. My father, who was an old man, slender and dark with the sun, tended his flock on the hill called Pnyka, above the plain of Attica and the city of Athens. The sheep and goats grazed between the cypress and olive trees, bleating in the bright days that bore my father gently toward the night. Eleven other shepherds worked the hill also, and my father was beloved among them. His was a sweet paternity, and the younger men would heed his advice. One morning, a young man approached my father as he steered his animals about. The beautiful stranger was such that at first my father could not discern if it was a boy or a girl. With the dawn sun at its back, the stranger addressed him, knowingly.

"Icarius, fond father of this slope . . ."

"I am he. Good morning, be welcome," my father said, extending his hand.

"I am grateful to you." When the stranger took Icarius' hand, the old man experienced a faint rolling and swelling in his loins, a sultry movement like an octopus in a cave of warmer water.

"I do not know you."

"My name is Dionysus, and I come to teach with the vine."

Icarius looked upon the radiant youth, whose hair was as black as coal and whose eyes shone like a swarm of bees in brilliant sunlight, all sparks and energies, and fell in beside him. They walked, and one of the goats nuzzled at Dionysus' hip.

"You know of the ichors that flow as blood in the veins of the immortals?" Dionysus began, and my father nodded like a sheep at the dun grass. "Within the grapes of the vine is such a liquor. He who drinks of it tastes, if you will, the blood of immortality, swims within it, and his spirit is disentangled from the petty snares of the earth. It is funny how the vines resemble traps and nooses, but through them is the transport to eternity. I am a teacher of the vine, and I have come to initiate you, if you would have me, Icarius."

As contented as my father had been, the opulent temptations shown him by Dionysus swayed him. "I would have you show me everything," he confessed to the radiant youth. And when he took communion with Dionysus, he felt the agility and promiscuity of a mountain goat start within him. He could traverse the crags of Pnyka with arrogance and haste. He felt himself potent as a black storm wheeling in a pale sky. While my father entreated the other eleven shepherds of the hill to know the truth of the vine also, Dionysus retired to a cave to masturbate.

But the shepherds awoke vomiting and with great pains in their brows, as though they had been struck with stones and briar. Their few possessions, their clothes and money purses, were somehow scattered about the slopes. "Icarius has poisoned us to steal our flocks!" they cried.

"The old man has betrayed us!"

When my father did not return home that night, I, Erigone, sat upright on my pallet in the darkness after the candles had burned down, unable to fight my terror and my tears. In the morning, I took my hound Maera, and we went into the hills to find my father.

We found his body, and the sound of our mourning screamed and howled down to the white streets of Athens. He had been pursued into the high crags and bludgeoned with stones and whipped with vines. His pitiful frame was contorted and broken open. His hair had been ripped from his scalp. Suddenly, I saw one of the shepherds crouching near a cypress tree. He was trying to wipe gore from his hands with grass.

"You did this, bastard!"

"No!" He denied it, and twice more as I ran toward him and was about to set Maera at his throat, he ran from me. I could not chase him, for I wanted to remain with my father.

Dionysus, who had heard our grief, awoke from his cave and tried to come to us, but he would be too late.

From the vines that had whipped my father, I fashioned a noose and threw it over a bough of the cypress tree. Standing upon a pile of grinding stones, I pushed my face through the noose, like a baby emerging from a womb. And I began to kick at the stones, making them fall away from me, until the rope bit my throat and I knew that I would die. Maera whimpered at my ankles, leapt and barked at me as I began to swing in the morning sunlight, cracking noises strangled from my throat. Then, the hound turned and raced toward the edge of the high crags and threw itself down to die.

When Dionysus found us, he was enraged. He set madness inside any woman who was wife, daughter, lover, or otherwise beloved of the eleven shepherds. Across the plain of Attica, women began to hang themselves in terrible contagion. They dropped like tears.

The Conning Tower

I left Magdalene's house and stepped outside into the raw street.

In that prurient night, Passover haunted the city like a flock of angry birds. Whatever the capricious nature of man toward man that was embedded in the split and struggling heart of Jesus of Nazareth, this was also in the Passover. The night when angels become vultures. It folded its wings around the city. A baby cried from an unlit room as I made my way. I shuddered to hear it. I was pleased that the next night would be the last time that we would have to endure this cruel feast. I was relieved to be apart from the others, but I knew that I would have to return to them. I felt like a ghost between the chill houses.

"Judas!" It seemed that my name was forever being called out from the darkness. I whipped about, finding myself surrounded by a pack of Roman soldiers, their black hair glistening in the torchlight borne by the man who led them. He stepped forward and I recognized him as Malchus, the slave-spy of Pontius Pilate. "We have come unarmed, Judas," he said. "Put away your knife." Malchus' red hair blazed.

"So, all of Pilate's premonitions have come to be. Look at us; we are like mirrors, you and I. We must have shared a body once."

"The knife, Judas, sheath it. I assure you, you see that our men have come without helmets or weapons. Pilate wishes for a reunion with you, and I think that you should oblige." Malchus swept his torch flames to illuminate his mob.

We went by a strange path through Jerusalem that took us through the Phrygian quarter. Fireworks exploded above us, raining lurid sparks. "It is the solstice, for the cult of Attis," Malchus explained with contempt. "The eunuch god! Look at this insanity." His lips curled into a snarl of repulsion. A date stall had been made into a temporary stage and was surrounded by naked men and women who crushed toward it. A tall eunuch cavorted above them. He held a hollow boar's head high in the full moonlight, and blackening blood poured from the stitches at its mouth and snout. The blood flushed down on the crowd, who cried out in pleasure, smearing the gore on their breasts and brows. "Attis baptizes with blood," said Malchus as another crude rocket detonated over the plaza. "Tomorrow, they will nail a mutilated effigy of their good shepherd to a pine tree. They will cut him down and seal him in a tomb. Priests will secretly remove the effigy, but at the end of the festival the disciples of Attis will return to the tomb, open it, and find the eunuch god vanished, resurrected and gone beyond. And spring will begin for the young Turks. They will gorge themselves on scented jellies and make for the hillsides to fuck each other. It is all a charade, but Pilate asks me to keep an eye on it. What good is a eunuch god? But what is a religion without genital mutilation, eh, Judas?"

"You seem to enjoy it, in your own way."

"Things are more intriguing since we are no longer stationed on the coast. Although, ironically, Pilate's promotion inland meant trading the mansion for a ship."

We found Pilate in the conning tower of the USS *Eldritch*.

High in the tower, Pilate lowered his rusting binoculars from watching the chaos outside and turned from the window to face me. He smiled and extended his hand to me. "Depressing, isn't it?" he said. As I made to shake his hand, Pilate took my wrists and turned my palms up, examining the broken glass scars there from when I escaped from the walled gardens of his mansion as a boy. "I see that you still bear the stigma of working for me."

The green lights of the instrument panels glowed about us as Pilate poured wine from a crystal decanter. A map of the city was projected upon a glass screen, and small clusters of light moved across it, showing the movements of different factions within Jerusalem. "We are enforcing the no-fly zone," Pilate announced wearily, "and are building more checkpoints around the city. The solstice is like a tinderbox, Judas. Jerusalem is a city of a thousand provocations. Do you know the only thing that I can do to keep a semblance of order here?"

"What?"

"I must shrug my shoulders. That is all I do, day and night. Malchus, you may leave us alone now. Go back to your studies."

"Sir." Malchus closed the heavy bomb door behind him.

"It strikes me, Judas, that power is indifference to suffering. You can drink, Judas; it's not poison or blood." Pilate laughed.

"So, I am not your prisoner?" I asked.

"I told you, I shrug my shoulders. I don't care that you betrayed my care of you, when I found you washed up and half-dead on my beach, over common gossip. And I am indifferent to your friend, Jesus of Nazareth." Pilate put his arm around my shoulders, and with his other hand, he gently moved my wine glass toward my lips. I drank as he went on. "But Jerusalem, whatever *Jerusalem* means, is not indifferent to him, even if he is content to arouse, obfuscate, confuse, and foment their little minds. It strikes me, also, that your friend is beginning to experience the indifference of tangible power. I hear that he discourages rich and poor in equal measure, that he is ambivalent and aloof, that he gives and takes offense arbitrarily. We have clear eyes and sensitive ears. And further, I *suspect* . . ." Pilate fell silent and put his finger to his pursed lips, as though he had finally discovered a way to articulate a problem that had long vexed him, and now, he wanted to chew and savor his inspiration.

"You suspect?"

"Judas, I suspect that this man seems not to be of his own mind, because you are behind everything that he does."

I shrugged my shoulders.

Pilate laughed again and poured us more wine, his brown eyes sparkling. "Oh, I'm not worried about a little dissent, here and there. This city feeds on dissent. What worries me is the extraordinary manner in which he is uniting people, not with him, but against him. I've never seen it like this. He assumes such immodest aristocracy for himself, not just over the whores of the city, but also over the entire world, that I fear a homicidal revolt against him. If I could hold him in the public balance against even the most venal criminal in Jerusalem, I can tell you that the crowd would be for the criminal, not Jesus."

I shrugged once more. I felt like a child without a ready answer to a worried father. But, finally, I asked him: "Why do you care so much about that to bring me here?"

"Judas, the point is that I don't care what happens to him. I care what happens to *you*. I have no children. When we found you as a boy in your wrecked skiff, I took you in as my drowned little fox. You were my page, but had you stayed, I wanted to make you my son. I know that Malchus attacked you and that he slandered you with lies that might have had you crucified. He was jealous, since he knew he would only ever be a slave in my retinue. His back is so deeply cut with welts and stripes from the lashing he received, he will never forget it. You were *different,* Judas, but we never had time." Pilate looked into my eyes, and I saw the tears in his. "I chanced upon an orphan, and he was taken from me by *doubt.* My fear is that a mob will come for your friend Jesus, and you and all of his allies will be murdered with him."

"What do you propose?"

"Let me take him in. Let me weigh him in public balance for the people."

"He already thinks that I will betray him."

"Then, you have nothing to lose. We can make it look as though you were not involved. If I can have him, then I might save the others. What do you say, Judas? One life for a dozen, or a thousand, is that so terrible?"

"I feel sick. I want no reward for this."

"None." Pilate agreed. He crossed the room to a water cooler and opened its chrome faucet. The water ran through his fingers and splashed the floor as he washed his hands. He filled a glass and handed it to me. "For your nausea, and our covenant."

I was not, as others would later ascribe in retrospect, a zealot or a political assassin. I was not a disillusioned revolutionary patriot, riven with conflict. These passions are superimposed upon me when men cannot accept that it is enough to act from experimental malice alone or to be a psychopath, however philosophical, driven by abstract desires, survival instincts, and a brutal sense of the world. Perhaps it did matter that I had been betrayed by Malchus and denied my rightful life with a new father in Pilate—another sentimental explanation. Cannot the killer be merely cruel? Must the inhumane be humanized and the beast rationalized? No, brother. The revolution will not be televised with a script by Gore Vidal wearing an embroidered bathrobe from a Mediterranean aerie, or broadcast to a soundtrack of blue-eyed soul on Clear Channel. It will not be mass-produced in air-port lounge editions or turned into a major motion picture. It will not be captured in the deteriorating paint job of Leonardo da Vinci, and my model will not be a small, misshapen black man with his elbow on the one-sided table. But as the moment of final betrayal drew near, had I been something other than apolitical, had I been more sentimental, then I might have anticipated the appalling threat that Jesus was about to pose to me.

THE LAST SUPPER

W hen I returned to Jesus and the disciples at the squat
they had made their home for the last days, my throat
was bruised from the asphyxiation from Magdalene and my
head was light from Pilate's wine. I told them that all the
money was gone. I was now treasurer of nothing but Jesus'
skin and bones, and even those I was about to surrender.

"I was worried," said Jesus. "The food does not matter. The
money is without consequence, only that you are here. We can
make a supper with the wine and sops of bread that we still have."

I told Jesus about what I had learned of Lazarus during the
night.

Jesus wept.

The following day was accelerated and compressed. We went
outside only briefly, but when we did, a woman clawed from
the gutter, tearing a fragment of Jesus' clothing to stanch her

nosebleed. I alone saw Jesus' lip curl in revulsion. It was as though she had stolen a part of his being, violated him, and blackened him with contamination. A blind man claimed to see him. Lepers rolled after us on creaking trolleys, so that Jesus quickened his step, even through the crowded bazaar. The aristocrat always experiences the common city as a crowd of corpses, animated, sightless things that still watch him as though transfixed by the radiance of the sun, a ball of lightning moving elegantly through their grotesque darkness. He was but another fantasy of the living dead.

That night, we made our last supper together. The atmosphere in the home we had taken in the red light district was solemn. We moved about one another as though ashamed. There was little food, and the oil lamps were weak.

"Look at us, retreated into this single black room," Jesus said as he poured the last of the wine into our cups. "We are like a king and his retinue, who have exhausted the palace. We are tired of going into the world, weary of hunting, filling our cellars, and slowly the world has died outside, taken over by thorny wilderness without our stewardship. We have gone from room to room, taking what we can, as the lights die, and we have no more treasure and no more food. We might be cringing inside a fractured boat, listening to the sharks circling us in the moonlight. This one lamp remains but is dying. There is a time of man when, inexplicably, his passion leaves him. Suddenly, the world promises nothing. And watching such a man, you might invent reasons for it. If you sing of it or whisper it with aches to a crowded auditorium, then it might seem tragic. But it is not. It is just *finished*."

"But, Rabbi," Simon Peter said, "what about what we have accomplished, and what is yet to be accomplished?"

"It has not worked. Look at us, how few we really are, how we are something in our minds that we are not as men." Jesus was sitting cross-legged on the dirt floor, a low table extending before him, at which we all sat. There were tears in his eyes. He stared at a beetle crawling across the wooden surface, its legs sticking in the wine spills. Jesus began tearing up a dry loaf of bread. "Each one of you that looks at me sees a different Lord, distorted by your own passion and manifold reflection. Here, if we bow our heads close to this beetle struggling in the wine, in the ripples we will all see him differently. Here he looks brittle, and here he resembles a mighty stag, and upon each you impose a mystery, something so humble that it must conceal great power, or something so powerful that it must conceal great humility. You do this to me. Those who wish me dead do this to me."

"Master, we are not the same as them!" Simon Peter protested.

"Yes, you are, but you do not know it."

"Then we cannot leave this room. It is as you said. This is the last room in the palace." Nathaniel sipped his wine with trembling lips.

"In the eyes of men, I am not so unlike the possessed man, Legion. My words confound as though they come from several tongues within the same mouth. Have none of you had doubt or experienced confusion?"

Silence.

"I came from sawdust and adultery," Jesus said. "Now, I am King. My kingdom is behind the stars, through the eye of the needle, beyond the veil of the Temple. But, if you know the stories of kings, you will know that kings' needs must be betrayed."

"No, my Lord!"

"It will be one of you. One closest to me." At this, there was a beat of wings, and a carrion bird landed heavily upon the roof, talons raking the dust.

Jesus filled a small basin with water from a pitcher that he had found in the strange house. Encircled by the disciples—Simon Peter and his half-blind brother Andrew with the gull-ripped eye, Philip the moon-face, Nathaniel who was without guile, Judas Thomas the taxidermist, Matthew the tax collector, James and John the sons of thunder, and silent James the son of Alphaeus, but without Jude Thaddeus or Simon the Zealot, who had gone to guerrilla war in Babylon—Jesus sat upon a studded casket. There, he began to discard his garments, which were stained with blood and soil. All eyes were upon him, fascinated. Beside the vines of blue veins in his wrist, I watched the rapid bulge of his pulse. When he was almost naked, Simon Peter made to hand him a clean white towel to cover himself. But Jesus took the towel to the basin and soaked it there. His narrow form wove through the half-light. Silently, he returned to his makeshift throne, the casket. I thought of Osiris locked in the iron maiden trap contrived by his brother Seth. I thought it right that Egyptian myths would surface and clash with Passover. With the drenched towel, Jesus began to wash the feet of those around me, and they protested.

"Lord, why do you wash my feet when I should wash yours?" Simon Peter asked.

Jesus said: "This is your exoneration. I can do this for you, but you cannot do this for me. Only I."

"But, Lord," Andrew's voice rose. "We do not wish to be separate from you."

"If this is not done," Jesus labored with his explanation, "you can have no part in me. Therefore, let me clean you. The master is the servant also."

"I am thinking of John the Baptist," Philip said, unfastening his threadbare sandals.

"Still, I say that one of you will lift his heel against me." At these words, they studied guiltily at their glistening feet, not seeing that Jesus had chosen not to wash mine. "Put your sandals back on. We must be ready to go out." Jesus gathered his clothes and dressed himself.

Nathaniel was able to make a broth. One fish head floated within it, one shocked eye staring from the grayish brine. As the bowl steamed over a lamp flame, it released a weak aroma. Then, I saw the sycophant Simon Peter leaning close to Jesus' breast, and then his mouth was at his ear. I shifted about the room and listened with extreme care to the whispering between them.

"Lord, Son of God, tell us of whom you speak. Who could betray you?"

And Jesus answered softly. "This morsel of bread, watch he to whom I give it after I have dipped it in the broth."

So, this was how my straw prince would seek to turn tables on me and to recast me at this final supper in the greatest of infamies. This I would not permit! Now, I took Jesus aside.

I remembered the child Jesus. I recalled standing in the desert with him and pretending that I was showing him a gilded kingdom as I pointed to a tempting blank space at the hot horizon. So desperate to please, he told me that he saw the kingdom that did not exist. This illusory kingdom he now inhabited fully. He would be the king of the unreachable, set upon a throne of my imagination. But, had not this perverse passion of his always been my intention and my fault?

Jesus knew it. And he was ashamed.

Here, he sought to manipulate me in his spiteful revenge. He had resolved to remove any sense of my will having been stronger than his. He was set to remove all moral agency from me. He sought to make a patsy of me. I gripped him by his skinny elbow, feeling the nub through his robes, and I led him into a shadowed corner. I did not take a morsel of bread with me. Instead, I had broken off a fistful, and I had pushed it into the boiling brine. Scales from the fish head clung to it as I stirred the eye about. In the salty scent, I thought of the symbols that Jesus had drawn in the sand for the fishermen, and I remembered being washed up on many shores.

"Judas, what is this?" Jesus was incredulous, yet a smile snaked across his lips as I forced the soddened bread into his hand and wiped my hand on his shoulder.

"It is the sop that you wished to pass to me. Outrageous fortune."

Jesus was shaken. He mouthed silently, searching for words.

"You were right, Jesus. I did bring you to this."

We stood together in the shadows.

Finally, Jesus said: "What you must do, do it quickly."

Jesus strode back to his waiting disciples. In their flattering presence, his words came fast, with determination that concealed his panic. His eyes flashed at each of them and at me. "This bread, you devour as if it were my flesh. This wine you drink, you swallow as if it were my blood. You will not forget this taste, this fear of betraying me. As I give, I renounce the body."

I heard the dogs, Gog and Magog, barking and yanking at their chains at either end of the street of whores. Sandaled feet scuffed in the street. Then, a bronze battering ram crashed against the door, sending splinters flashing into the room, but the furniture piled behind the door held it firm for a moment. A young Roman legionnaire called from the street. "Nazarene! Come out! You have broken into this house! In the name of Pilate, we have come to arrest you!" The battering ram came again. I took Jesus' arm, dragging him to his feet and pulling him toward the small door at the back of the house. All of us ran outside, into the sweat of the Jerusalem night. They had followed me.

THE PASSION OF JUDAS

In Gethsemane, beneath the gibbous moon, Jesus and his disciples felt themselves lost within the dolorous trees and no longer heard the metal pursuit of the Romans, or the black cloaks of the Sanhedrin, or the rage of the Pharisees, or the tumult of the multitudes whom Jesus observed from his new aristocracy. They had been forced to the last corner of the garden. I had seen the olive and cypress trees of the Garden of Gethsemane many times before, in the premonitions of Cyborea, the woman who claimed to be my mother in Kerioth, and in the oily vortices of Vincent van Gogh, where all was dread and the solipsistic curls of impending self-murder. In the midst of the night, I felt the oil beneath his feet, smearing through the grass and fallen red blossom. I plucked at one of the branches, and a trail of blood ran into my sleeve and toward my breast. The flight from the barricaded hovel had left some of the disciples euphoric at having escaped so narrowly. They lay back upon the ground and laughed with relief, their chests rising and falling hard and heavy. But soon they heard Jesus' despair and were much afraid. They went near to him, half-concealing themselves like guilty shades behind the black trees, listening. And they saw that I was kneeling beside him.

"I know that it seems that I have been weeping for so much of my life, Judas, but my thoughts and my heart are heavy as millstones and always have been so. I live with despair upon despair, and I cannot find the kernel of it inside me."

And Jesus stood up, staggering slightly, and gripped one of the olive trees for support, swinging there for a moment before collapsing to his knees again, like an actor working a stage. A noise came from his throat. The disciples gathered about him in the swollen dirt.

The sons of Zebedee urged him, "Despair not, my master."

"It is more than despair," he answered. "It is a passionate chasing of death."

"Help us to understand what we are to do, for we would follow you to prisons and unto death, even."

"No, this is not so. You would not." The disciples were wounded by these words. Simon's cheekbones shone with brilliant tears.

"Lord, I am ready."

"No, Simon. The cockerel will not crow this morning until you have thrice denied that you know me. The morning star will hang in the dawn, and Lucifer will sift you aside like wheat."

"He will fail, Lord!"

"No, he will not. So, I have prayed for you, that you will turn away from him again and make these others stronger." And then Jesus clawed against the olive tree and rose to his feet. "I say unto you all, when I stripped you of your possessions, when you were without a purse, without sandals, did you lack anything?" His pointed finger moved from man to man.

"Nothing."

"Now, you will need these things again. Take back your purse from the nail where you hung it in your darkened home, far away. Take up your sword. If you lack a sword, then buy one."

I wondered at the continual reversals and strange mirrors in my brother's mind.

"We will," they said, but they were wracked with confusion and doubt. Yet, Jesus' permission for them to carry money and swords and to assimilate with the middle class also gave them great relief. "Between us we have two swords and will buy more." The disciples, who were exhausted, lay down to rest in the moonlight.

Jesus tried to smile, but a spectral agony was at work within him. He withdrew from them, but I shadowed him. Jesus prayed, and his tears fell upon the soil, heavy as blood from his eyes.

"Father, if you are willing, please take this cup from me. Still, I know that it is not my will that moves the world. If you will not remove the cup, if the only way for me to be rid of it is to drink it down, then I will."

And I whispered "Drink, Jesus."

"They are golden in the moonlight, like a cadre of angels."

It was Malchus and Pilate's soldiers.

My mouth moved inside the needles of his beard, not to identify him—because by this time, everyone knew Jesus of Nazareth by his somnambulant walk and dreaming words— but to *inspire* him for the last time, to breathe the remnants of my passion into him, and to finish what we had begun when we were children, to give him the strength to finish it. His brown eyes, as whorled and abandoned as snail shells, were closed, his pungent mouth disbelieving as the serpent of my breath hissed through his aching teeth, then passed over his tongue, into the shining purses of his flesh. I brought him here, constructed him from fleece, bone, blood, dust, wine, seed, straw, my occluded desires, my orphanage, the endless art of my fury. His disciples, his ineffectual mirrors, shivered between the soldiers and the knotted trees of Gethsemane. By this time, he could not resist anything that I suggested to him. It had been that way for so long that I did not have to witness him being led away.

Malchus reached inside his red cloak and tossed something at me. From reflex, I could not prevent my hand from reaching up to catch it before it struck me in the face. Malchus' eyes glowed with jealousy and ancient hatred. The purse hit my hand, and my fingers closed around it. The coins inside it rattled like bones. I struck fast with my dagger, cutting off Malchus' ear, and he fell to the ground howling in a foxy arc of blood.

"Bastard, I wanted no reward!"

"Judas!" The voices of the disciples rose against me.

Lightning struck in the black sky.

And I bolted.

THE TRIAL OF JESUS

True to his word, Pilate was to weigh Jesus in the public balance. First, Jesus was brought before Pilate and Herod. High in the conning tower, Herod's chair hovered on a cushion of steam jets as he considered the man standing before him, between the glowing instrument panels of the *Eldritch*. As Luke tells it, Herod had Jesus arrayed in gorgeous apparel, for such was his humor. Herod hovered closer. "I fear," he began, before sipping at his bloody wine, "that as my rule grows longer in experience, so that experience of the world becomes more repetitive. Are we to have another John the Baptist on our hands, Pilate?" And then, to Jesus, he asked: "They say that you are the King of the Jews. Is that so, carpenter's son?"

"You have said it."

"You are the very Son of God? Will you do us no sign, commit no miracle?" This, Jesus did not answer.

Herod grew impatient. "Oh, why must they be so obtuse? Their world hangs in the balance. Not even the fate of the universe can make them speak plainly. Still, you call others satanic? Can this kingdom of yours not withstand truth and direct address? Is not the rule of Herod emphatic? Could you not take a leaf from my book, Nazarene? I tell you that your circumlocutions are the real sin against man. Smoke and mirrors. The sheep need a dog! Let us discover what the people think of this King of the Jews. Bring him out, Pilate." They took Jesus upon the deck of the aircraft carrier and another man also, an anarchist named Barabbas.

"Barabbas," Pilate mulled, "tell me, what does the name Barabbas mean?"

The prisoner, who was covered in the excrement of his confinement and gory with tortures, replied through his broken teeth and tar-black beard: "It means Son of the Father."

"Then," Pilate said to Herod, "we cannot win." Herod returned to the interior of the conning tower.

Pilate took up a microphone to address the crowd that assembled far below, all about the hull of the landlocked vessel that controlled the city. Herod could hear the trial outside on the deck and the mob surrounding the ship calling out for Barabbas. Alone in the metal room, listening to the dim pulse of the sonar, Herod told himself: "It is accomplished."

When Pilate returned, he shrugged and lowered the microphone, letting it swing on its rubber cable.

I watched the trial from within the mob. Spoilt fruit pelted the hull of the ship. The Romans held the roaring crowd back with lances and shields. I too cried out for Barabbas, holding in my mind's eye the image of Jesus conniving to destroy me with his pathetic morsel of bread and whispering with Simon Peter. I saw Pilate strutting with his microphone, playing up the drama of the trial for the crowd, resplendent in his Roman livery, and I was struck by what might have been. Mary Magdalene was there somewhere, selling bags of peanuts. Barabbas was set free. Jesus was sentenced to be crucified and was to be taken to the hill Golgotha, the place where we had met as children.

JUDAS ISCARIOT AND THE SCAPEGOAT

I n the tattered aftermath, I returned to the wreckage of Akeldama, the field of blood, the place where two brothers had sought to annihilate the evidence of their former degradation, washing the base clay from their hands. So it had been with Jesus and I, Judas. I had with me the same amount of money as the urn-makers had possessed when they made their escape: thirty pieces of silver. The sun that was a coin of blood rose slowly, and vultures flew over the distant place of skulls, where the bulldozers worked at the landfill of flesh. Red dirt and smashed clay extended all about me. The rain had opened cracks in the earth, and a thousand worms had split out from it to eat, and in turn ravens fell upon them.

The money weighed heavy with me as I held the final portrait of Jesus in my mind. I had delivered him. His skin had been flayed from him, his head had been shaved, and his loins were black from beatings. He had gone through the uneven streets, scourged and insulted. At Akeldama, I could still hear the creak of the rope as his cross was hauled upright and the grinding before it fell into its socket, and the cracking of his ribs as his weight fell forward and down, asphyxiating him. I wondered if it was one of the crosses that his father had made for the Romans. Joseph the carpenter had made no appearance for his son's death. Before he reached the summit of Golgotha, still in the labyrinthine streets, Mary, his mother, had forced her face between the brawling lines of soldiers and citizens, but when she called out to him, he did not know her. High on the crucifix, he endured in the rain, crying out to the impenetrable sky. One of the soldiers thrust his lance between Jesus' heaving ribs to finish him. And for his ineffable kingdom, which I had convinced him of, there was a crown of thorns wrapped about his bald and bloody head. There was a wooden sign nailed above him bearing a single word that had been scratched into the grain with a dagger and illuminated with waste from his own body.

IRONY.

In the rising sun and the shadows cast by the remaining storm clouds, I saw a movement at the horizon. It was moving painfully, inexorably, toward me. I wiped the sweat from my eyes and tried to make it out more clearly. At first, I thought it to be a man. Then it was close enough for me to make out its form. The goat struggled across the wasteland, its front legs buckling as it stumbled in the awful earth. Sometimes it appeared white and sometimes black as the clouds, and strange light traced across it. I began to walk across the field toward the animal, loosening the gourd at my belt to find water for it. I

remembered him. His left hind hoof was misshapen. His hair
was pale with strokes of copper. There was a rope around his
neck, so that I was able to pull him to the shade of the single
cypress tree that grew in the field, surrounded by the red dirt.
I held the water, and the goat sucked at the nozzle, drinking
for its life. For some hours, I sat beneath the tree, and the goat
lay with its head in my lap. Mine would be the self-murder
about which all others would be reconsidered. I was in posses-
sion of myself for the last time.

When it was time, I took the rope from the neck of the
goat and fixed the purse of silver pieces to its horns instead.
I stared one final time into the coin slots of its eyes before it
left me there.

*   *   *

JUDAS WAS dreaming, and the soil fell tightly over the
world. He would stagger up against the trees laden with
black insects and small heat and lurch toward collapse. Move
through the rope, eyebrows and beard. Move through the
rope into fury. Exhibit the burbles of a vicious smile, the soil
screaming, the sky a dense inversion of sun and moon, the
cypress dead at the roots. He stretched, breathing, yanking
the lifelike flesh skillfully wrapped around his neck, and swallowed. His anger eclipsed everything. It eclipsed everything
that had been said in streams of sweat and blood. Fire drank
the light, the darkness like a wrinkled mouth around him,
his genius and his odor falling limpidly from him, from his
armpits, the pit of his groin, abandoned. His steaming neck
moved through the rope, dissolved the Temple in a sheer

outcry of love and wretchedness, one-half of the crucified, causing the same effect. He left them behind and set himself against their vineyards and fig trees and the mountain of their will. Silently they forced him. And saying this, imagining himself struggling like a butterfly against being a spy in the grove, he looked around. His sweat came, and he growled to beat it down. The brain is trapped in the bone as a hungry jackal muffled in the rubble of Brooklyn. Who had been running after him?

Memories of solitude and then not of solitude, light passing over his forehead as he shuddered. Bare feet dangling over worms, his cock spiritless, letting go. The stars were strings of stains. He was not afraid.

Look at it: his neck fleshed out, tightening his belt, suspended, budding; one gigantic voice reaching into his feet, hanging, jumping through his noose and neck. His neck is a work of art. It is a testament to the sound of the desert. Judas had been in the desert alone, bare feet dangling over. The goats shifted masks, nuzzling wet pigment.

The stars were strings of stains. He was not afraid.

JUDECCA

I, Judas, am the paragon of suicides.
I, Judas, am the ghost hand of your faith.
I, Judas, am your suspended disbelief.

Lucifer was there, his immense torso projecting from the ice of Judecca, like a man waist deep in arctic water. Even from a distance, he was colossal, surrounded by hundreds of frozen corpses that draped the cold, impenetrable slabs. The permanent ice held him and was made thicker by his tears as his gargantuan wings beat weakly, torn and bloodied where he tried to free himself. At the center of the earth, his wings cast one final shadow of futility.

I beheld the goat horns that grew from the brow of his leonine head, bowed in the half-light of the cavern. The rope of his red hair ran over his shoulders. I witnessed the churning of faces in the glassy ice beneath my feet as my crampons bit the surface. My presence there unleashed a siren scream as the corpses on the slabs began to split open like stitched mouths breaking their twine, coiling blue-black entrails over the frost, and the spectral noise reverberated in the halls of all death.

Lucifer looked up.

In the muscular vortices of his fists he gripped the decapitated corpses of the traitors Brutus and Cassius, their legs flapping like rubber. I thought of Malchus and imagined pushing my revolver into the soft plate of his mouth. I pictured the muzzle flash suppressed by his tongue, a shard of his skull exploding off like smashed bloody crockery, and his corpse falling silently into a transparent ravine. Lucifer's mouth chewed the heads of the traitors like an obscene child chewing a pair of dolls. He closed his teeth on their hair and let them hang there. A tar of black lipstick slipped from the maw that called me like a return to an unknowable womb. I made my way across the ice, breathing in the stench of he who died as slow as a star, Lucifer, from the back of the heavens.

The pain in my throat increased from the effort of breathing again. Lucifer's breath came like a storm. The smell of it was the same as the smell of the rope that I had taken from the animal to make my death and my transfiguration. He reached down to me and opened his bloody fingers. His long nails scraped and whined across the permafrost.

| ABOUT THE AUTHOR |

JAMES REICH is a writer and co-founder of post-punk band
Venus Bogardus. He appears in fictionalized form as "Jude" in
Julie Powell's memoir *Julie & Julia.* He was born in England
and relocated to New Mexico in 2009. He is currently a con-
tributing faculty member at Santa Fe University of Art and
Design and is at work on his second novel.

| ACKNOWLEDGMENTS AND PERMISSIONS |

THE AUTHOR gratefully acknowledges the support and wisdom of Will Lippincott, Christina Shideler, Jack Shoemaker, and Dan Smetanka.

With thanks to Alastair Brotchie for his kind permission to quote from Jacques Rigaut's *Lord Patchogue & Other Texts*. Translated by Terry Hale, Atlas Press, London, 1993.

This novel is dedicated to Hannah and our family.

Printed in the United States
by Baker & Taylor Publisher Services